SILURID

GERRY GRIFFITHS

SEVERED PRESS
Hobart Tasmania

SILURID

WWW.SEVEREDPRESS.COM

ISBN: 978-1-925493-61-0

DEDICATION

For Frank, Dale, and Leonard
The place isn't the same without you guys
And for Hannah and Summer
May you be waiting for us on Rainbow Bridge

AUTHOR'S NOTE

I have always been a tremendous fan of the literary conflict of *man versus nature*, or to be more concise, *man against beast*. Two of my all-time favorite novels are Herman Melville's classic *Moby Dick* and Peter Benchley's thriller *Jaws*. I especially love John Huston and Steven Spielberg's superb film adaptations.

As exciting and terrifying as these stories are, the impending danger created by these cunning and tenacious monsters was only a threat to those foolish enough to venture into the water.

Just about everything you are about to read in *Silurid* is true; with the exception of the *KHIP news station*, the *Madison levee* and the nearby town, the *Murdock Fish Hatchery*, and *Lake Recluse*, which are figments of my imagination; as are the *silurid monsters*—to the best of my knowledge.

Gerry Griffiths
June 2016

PART ONE

THE SILURID RESULT

CHAPTER ONE

Lake Recluse—Northern California—1997

Devon McNeeley sped away from the Alpine lake's shoreline, traveling the frontage road in his golf cart. He pressed the accelerator to the floor in hopes of squeezing enough juice out of the battery to get up a steep hill. Instead of picking up speed, the golf cart slowed and labored up the incline.

Max sat contently by his side in the passenger seat. The golden retriever stuck its nose in the air and sniffed the morning scents. His wet, leathery tongue dangled out of the corner of his mouth like a pink strip of luncheon meat.

Devon waved, passing the shack at the main gate.

Kelly Baron, a part-time employee, paused to return the salutation before handing a day pass to the driver in a white minivan.

Kelly was taking night classes to get her beautician license. Most of the time she practiced on herself. Devon had to laugh. This morning, her hair was a weird shade of blue.

The golf cart picked up speed when the road leveled off. Veering off onto a dirt patch, Devon hit the brakes in front of a long row of mailboxes.

Max jumped out to explore.

Devon reached into the McNeeley mailbox and pulled out a curled tube of envelopes, magazines, and junk mail flyers. He browsed through the mail, frowning at one of the correspondences. He tore open the flap on the envelope. He removed the folded letter, spread it open, and browsed the contents.

"Give me a break, will you?" he shouted and slammed his palm on the steering wheel. He stuffed the letter into his denim shirt pocket.

"Max! Here boy." Devon spun the golf cart around, but Max was nowhere to be seen.

Devon gazed up a nearby hillside dotted with manzanita and sagebrush.

He could hear Max rooting inside the brush.

"Max! Let's go!"

Max scampered down the hill, bits of twigs and pollen matting his coat. After a brisk shake, the dog leaped up onto the blue, vinyl seat, panting as if he had just completed a strenuous run.

Devon decided to take the service road before checking in at the store. He turned left and gunned the cart down the hill. The onrush of air made Max's jowls flap comically, exposing his pink and black gums.

Being the off-season, the resort was mostly deserted except for the few retired residents that lived on the lake all-year round. It was disheartening for Devon to see so many *For Sale* signs as they went down the road. He passed vacated, lavish doublewide mobile homes, and run-down trailers and fifth wheels on weedy roadside lots.

Liz Fallow was still in her housecoat and slippers, dutifully tending to her limp azaleas and gardenias in front of her modest trailer. Stony-faced gnomes, miniature windmills, and giant plastic sunflowers adorned the flowerbeds. Rosie, Liz's English springer spaniel, was sitting at the base of the porch steps, giving the back of her head a vigorous scratch with her hind foot.

"Morning, Liz," Devon greeted.

"Good morning to you, young man," Liz answered back.

Rosie yelped excitedly.

Max replied with a forceful bark.

"Down, you big stud," Devon said, waving to Liz as he drove by.

Devon spotted his younger brother, Sean, hiking up from the shore. The fourteen-year-old, though reluctant at times, generally helped with the chores around the resort. Shouldering his compound bow equipped with a fishing reel, Sean had a bountiful stringer. It was a shame that they were only carp.

For years, Lake Recluse had been famous for its game fish. The lake had been abundant with German browns, rainbows, largemouth and smallmouth bass, bluegills, and catfish. Then, for some unexplained reason, carp started showing up at the end of fishermen's hooks. No one knew exactly where the dreaded bottom feeder had come from. Wasn't long before the other species began to dwindle because the carp fed on their roe and fingerling offspring. Game fishermen stopped coming. No one was going to boast about reeling in an oversized goldfish no matter how large it was.

Sean ran up the steps to one of the trailers.

There was a resident sign carved on a wooden plaque hanging under the patio: *Stone's Abode.*

Sean dumped the stringer of garbage fish into a washtub by the front door.

"Come on, I'll give you a lift," Devon called out as he pulled up. He shooed Max into the cargo space.

Just then another golf cart pulled up alongside Devon.

The driver's belly just cleared the lower part of the steering wheel. He had a ruddy scar that ran down the left side of his face and was missing the last two fingers on his left hand.

"Morning, gents," Jasper Joyner greeted and took a slug of his beer. He crushed the can and tossed it on the catchall shelf under the dash. He reached into his cooler and retrieved another beer.

"Starting a little early, aren't we, Jasper?" Devon caught the pungent aroma of stink bait and body odor and tried not to wrinkle his nose.

"Just putting a perspective edge on the day," Jasper replied. He reached into the crinkled bag squished between his legs and shoved a handful of crumbly barbecue potato chips into his mouth, most of which ended up on the front of his San Francisco 49ers T-shirt.

In the back of Jasper's golf cart were two more ice chests, four fishing poles, a folded lawn chair, an umbrella, and a minnow bucket.

"Well, if it isn't Mr. Fancy Pants," Jasper said, acknowledging the man walking on the road towards them.

Claude Talbert was carrying a light fly rod in one hand, a pair of chest waders in his other hand. He wore a British tweed hat with tiny handmade flies hooked around the band. His plaid shirt was buttoned all the way up and tucked inside the waistband of a pressed pair of gray, wool trousers. A French-Reed creel hung off his shoulder. He looked the proper gentleman, puffing on his pipe.

"Any luck?" Sean asked, running over to the fly fisherman.

"Luck is never a factor," Claude nobly replied. He opened the lid of the creel to give Sean a peek.

"Holy cow, Claude has a couple German browns."

"Wow, no one's caught a German brown around here for ages," Devon said.

"Don't let him bullshit you, Devon. He probably got them at the store. Isn't that right, Claude?" Jasper laughed.

"Whatever you say."

"See. He won't even deny it."

"At least I play a fair game and don't go around gagging the fish with those rancid concoctions you fondly call bait."

"Beats whipping that line back and forth all day. Personally, I like to kick back and enjoy myself when I fish, thank you very much. Well, I guess I'll see you all tonight," Jasper said, and drove off in his cart.

"Schmuck," Claude said and blew out a bluish ring of cherry-blend smoke.

"Where'd you catch them, if you don't mind me asking?" Devon asked.

"Well, Devon, all I can say is that I did not get them at the market."

"I thought as much," Devon said, and smiled. He waved to Sean to get in and they drove off to the store.

The country store was small with two large paned windows facing out onto the parking lot. A Neon Budweiser sign hung in one window, a Coors sign in the other. There were faded snapshots taped to the windows of fishermen with their catches back when the lake was bountiful. A service window was just around the left side of the building for taking lunch orders and passing out food. Five picnic tables with benches were tucked under a red and white striped awning.

Devon hadn't quite stopped when he pulled up to the parking stall by the entrance door when Max vaulted out of the cargo space. The dog bolted for the park bench to the right of the door. The bench was Max's favorite spot. He jumped up, sprawled on the bench, and rested his head on his paws.

"Better see if Mom has any rentals lined up," Devon said, climbing out of the cart.

"Gotcha." Sean went inside the store.

The season had been slow at the resort mostly due to the poor fishing. No one was willing to drive two or three hours to catch carp. The meat of the fish could be boiled for two days and still have the texture of rubber, not to mention tasting like crap. Devon often kidded Sean that whoever came up with the name *carp* was dyslexic.

Devon suspected that the other resorts and campgrounds like Shasta and Clear Lake had attracted their business.

Sean strolled out of the store.

"Mom is finishing with a customer. I'm going down to get a boat ready," he said. "Come on, Max."

Max leaped from the bench and trotted after Sean, heading down to the dock where ten aluminum rental boats were moored.

A minivan—the same vehicle Devon had seen at the main gate—was parked beside the McNeeley's GMC pickup.

A bell over the door rang softly as Devon entered the store.

Most of the shelves on the four aisles were stocked with canned foods, packaged dry goods, and glass jars of preservatives and condiments.

One row of shelves was devoted to fishing tackle: hooks, sinkers, fillet knives, hook removers, floats, tackle boxes, stringers, spools of fishing line, and jars of Power Bait. A magazine stand and two clothes racks with T-shirts and tank tops with zippy slogans, shorts, and swim trunks were at the end of one aisle.

The back wall housed the glass door refrigeration units sparsely stocked with bottled and canned drinks, bait, and bags of ice.

Fishing rods of all types—bamboo poles, graphite poles, and Ugly Sticks—were affixed to the walls on eyehooks. There were more pictures—these framed for prosperity—of record catches. Trophy trout and largemouth bass were expertly preserved in shellac, mounted on shiny plaques with tiny bronze plates identifying the size and date of each catch.

The register was up front along with a glass counter stocked with Mitchell, Zebco, Shimano, Penn, and other popular brand reels.

Nell, Devon's eight-year-old sister, was sitting at a small table in the corner behind the glass counter. She was earnestly printing in a spiral notebook, her tiny fist wrapped around a #2 pencil. A large book was open on the table, and by the colorful illustrations on the pages, Devon knew Nell was doing her geography lesson.

Devon's mother, Kate, had taken on the task of tutoring both Nell and Sean at home. As the resort was secluded and demanded much of her attention, Kate could not afford devoting three hours a day driving the kids to and from the nearest public school.

Kate was behind the counter, filling out a rental agreement.

She was wearing a green blouse, jeans, and a rugged pair of work boots. Her auburn hair flowed just over her shoulders, and while in her mid-forties, Kate was attractive, business-smart, and not to be reckoned with. She had raised her two sons and daughter by herself as Devon's father, a trucker by trade and a scoundrel by nature, had drifted out of their lives shortly after Nell was born.

After a time, they had all adjusted to not having a husband or father around.

A man and his son were browsing about the store.

"There, Mr. Linton, if you would just sign here, the boat should be just about ready," Kate said, placing the pen on the paperwork.

Mr. Linton was staring at the map of the lake on the wall.

"This is our first time here. Could you tell us a little bit about the lake?"

"Sure, I'd be delighted." Kate walked around the counter and joined Mr. Linton.

"Lake Recluse has a surface area of 3,500 acres and 45 miles of shoreline. Not big enough to get lost on but big enough to find some solitude if you like. The resort consists of sixty-three mobile homes, all situated here at Recluse Cove." Kate pointed to where the mobile homes were on the map.

"Up here is Adobe Creek, which has been dried up for the past fifty-some years. This is Chickaree Creek. The creek feeds the lake with snowmelt from the Sierra Range during the spring.

"There are numerous islands on the lake, most of them sandbars, with the largest being Grizzly Island. There's nothing really there but an old oak tree that refuses to die. Along this shore is the service road that leads to the boat ramp, marina and boat docks, and this is where we are, the country store. Farther down is Landon Cove. And here are the campgrounds," Kate said, pointing with her finger.

"We might check the campgrounds out later," Mr. Linton said. "What's this at the end of the lake? It says *dam*, but I never knew there was a dam up here."

"Dates back to FDR and the New Deal," Kate said, refusing Mr. Linton with a smile when he offered her a stick of chewing gum before giving his son one.

"You mean back in the 30s?"

"That long ago. The Works Progress Administration wanted to build a dam on Lake Recluse—even wanted to call it Roosevelt Dam. The runoff from the lake would feed into a tributary that would have connected to the Sacramento River and down to the San Francisco Bay."

"I didn't know that," Mr. Linton confessed.

"Only the dam was never finished."

"Why was that?"

"Are you familiar with the town Madison?"

"That's where we're from."

"Oh. Well, it seems that the dam project was doomed from day one. Those two circles on the map next to the dam site are excavation caves that were never completely dug out because the workers struck granite harder than their picks.

"So, they shifted the site, but before they were able to finish pouring the foundation, the project was put on hold so that the men could be sent up to Madison to build a levee. Once the levee was built, the only source into Lake Recluse was cut off, that being Adobe Creek.

"There was no need to complete the dam, so the only part built was a single diversion tunnel that stands useless above the lake. Some bitter old-timers refer to the site as Damn Franklin. We just call it Franklin Dam," Kate said and returned to the counter.

"Interesting," Mr. Linton said and turned to his son. "Kevin, here's a dollar. Go pick out something for yourself while Daddy pays for the boat."

The boy, a year or two younger than Nell, ran down the aisles in search of candy.

"Mr. Linton, if you'd like to sign here," Kate said.

The man came over to the counter, handed Kate the money, and signed the rental agreement.

"The deposit will be refunded once you return the boat."

"I understand. I'll be right back. I have to get something out of the car," Mr. Linton said and exited the store.

Kevin raced back, grinning like a miner who had just struck pay dirt.

"Are these Gummy Bears?" he asked, holding up a package of purple worm lures.

"No, dummy, that's for catching fish," Nell said, laughing from across the counter.

"Nell! Behave. Now scoot, back to your studies young lady," Kate said.

"But Mom. I'm done."

"Then I'll get 'em for my dad. Here." Kevin handed Kate his dollar.

Devon watched Kate take the $4.98 package of purple worms and ring up the sale on the register for one dollar and place the bill in the till.

"You tell your daddy these were on sale, okay?" Kate told him.

"I will."

"Also, if you want these to work, tell your daddy to cast toward the shore when you're out in the boat. Can you remember that?"

"I think so."

The front door opened, and Mr. Linton poked his head in.

"Kevin, let's go, son."

"Bye bye," Kevin said and scurried out the door.

"Mom, I wish you wouldn't just give things away," Devon said.

"Since when do we allow our purse strings to close our hearts? Devon? Is something wrong?" Kate asked when she saw the strained expression on her son's face.

"We got another letter from the Bureau of Land Management. This time, they're threatening to terminate our lease."

Kate came out from behind the counter. Devon felt her hand gently touch his shoulder.

"We'll get through this."

"I wish I could believe that."

"Devon, this isn't like you. What's the matter?"

"Nothing."

"Is it Jess again?"

"Can we just drop it?"

"What happened between you two?" Kate asked.

"I guess we're just got too busy to have a relationship. What with me trying to keep this damn place afloat, and her, running that stupid hatchery."

"Surely, you two can—"

"I've got work to do," Devon said and stormed out of the store wishing his mother would learn to let up and quit badgering him about Jess.

9

CHAPTER TWO

Jess Murdock exited Interstate 5 onto the Madison turnoff and looped her black Bronco XLT onto the frontage road. Groves of olive trees stood to the right in perfect alignment. On the left was Madison levee running as far as the eye could see.

Up ahead, the angry clouds bullied the darkening sky.

Last night, the rain had come down so hard that Jess had not slept well.

Normally, the sound of the rain drumming on the roof and the windowpanes of her cottage would have lulled her off to sleep, but instead, she had tossed and turned worrying how the rain was affecting the hatchery.

She turned her attention to the news broadcast on the radio.

"More debris flows and mudslides threaten the town of Madison. Four homes suffered major damage last night when the hillside behind the properties suddenly gave way. Luckily, no one was hurt. Well, Bob, any relief from El Nino?"

"I'm afraid not, Beverly. The Weather Service is predicting new records this year, surpassing those established over a century ago. So far, we have had one hundred and two days of consecutive rainfall. Expect patchy clouds today with more rain in the forecast for this afternoon. Back to you, Beverly."

The female newscaster did a short plug for the upcoming President's Day sale at Madison Hardware before turning the airways over to Chris Rea singing *The Road to Hell.*

Jess checked her speed and the time, not wanting to be late for the tour. The stop at the chemical store had taken longer than she had anticipated. The rain had saturated the ponds, causing an algae bloom, so she had picked up ten sacks of copper sulfate to control the plankton growth. The new warehouseman had taken forever writing up the order, searching in the back, and loading the sacks into the back of the Bronco.

She edged the speedometer needle five miles over the speed limit.

A black sedan meandered in front of her. She drummed her fingers impatiently on the steering wheel and was forced to slow down.

"Come on, slowpoke. I don't have all day." Jess was considering passing but quickly changed her mind when she spotted a logging truck barreling toward her in the opposing lane. She bided her time, watching the driver of the sedan through the car's rear window. The man had a cellular phone pressed against his ear. She hated drivers who dawdled on the road, talking to who-knows-who, oblivious to the other cars around them.

The logging truck shook the Bronco as it thundered by. Two cars followed behind the big rig's draft. A bend in the road cut off her view of any opposing traffic.

Tired of waiting, Jess stomped on the accelerator. The 351 horsepower engine responded with a muffled roar. She steered around the sedan, gave the driver a scowl, and was about to return her attention to the road when she heard the jarring blare of an air horn.

Jess looked out the windshield and saw the fast approaching grill of another logging truck.

"Shit!"

She gunned the Bronco and swerved back into her lane, cutting in front of the sedan by mere feet, just missing the truck speeding by, the force of the big rig almost buffeting her off the road.

She glanced back in her review mirror. The driver of the sedan seemed unfazed, talking on his phone.

"Asshole!"

A flagman stood in the middle of the road and thrust out his STOP sign.

Jess felt her blood pressure creep up a notch.

She braked, bringing the Bronco to a halt behind a maroon Mustang. Higher than the car in front of her, Jess had a clear view of the Caltrans workers in their orange vests and hard hats, busily off-loading sandbags from a flatbed truck. Two yellow bulldozers ran the metal teeth of their scoops up against the embankment of the levee.

A narrow channel of water seeped from the base of the levee, forming a stream that crossed over the frontage road. The stream poured down into a wide ditch carved through an abandoned field that ran behind the Murdock Fish Hatchery. The gully had once been Adobe Creek.

Jess watched a burly man climb out of a parked truck. Toting a small case, he began climbing the steep bank of the levee. She recognized the emblem on his truck door and figured he was a hydrologist technician from the U.S. Geological Survey going up to take measurements.

On the other side of the levee was the Sacramento River. Almost 400 miles long, the Sacramento River flowed down California's backbone, originating near Mount Shasta and emptying into the San Francisco Bay. Part of the river's journey grazed the banks of the Madison Levee. The Sacramento River had swollen from the constant rains already flooding other communities nestled too close or with elevations below the river.

Madison was on flood alert.

The flagman turned his sign around to SLOW and signaled for the traffic to pass.

The Mustang edged through the water. The rear tires squealed then regained traction on the dry pavement.

Jess waved to the flagman and proceeded on. She turned right at the sign, *Welcome to the Murdock Fish Hatchery*, and drove along the gravel road.

She could see much of the hatchery out the passenger window through the chain-link fencing. A tall, sixty-foot long windowless Quonset hut and a one-acre pond occupied a corner of the property. A separate security fence—made of twelve-foot-high cinderblock and topped with impenetrable razor wire coils— protected the rear of the hut and pond from intruders.

Beyond were sixty concrete raceways, each one teeming with trout and bass.

Behind the raceways were the aeration building, the aeration ponds, the equipment shed, and four one-acre ponds stocked with catfish.

Jess turned into the hatchery's gravel lot and parked in front of the office next to the visitor center.

She was glad to see a few cars in the lot and checked her watch, relieved that she still had five minutes before the tour was due to begin. She pulled into her stall and turned off the ignition. She jumped out of the Bronco and raced around to the rear of the vehicle. Pressing down on the release bar, she swung the spare tire carrier out. She inserted the key into the lock, unrolled the window, reached inside and pulled down the tailgate.

"Billy, can you get these for me?" Jess shouted to the man driving up in a battery operated flatbed utility cart. Billy Garner, her foreman, headed up a crew of five maintenance men. He had a stubbly gray beard and was lean and grisly.

Jess adored Billy more than her real father.

"Sure thing, Jess," Billy replied. He stopped the cart then stiffly climbed out of the cab. "I tell you, if this rain doesn't let up soon, my joints are going to lock up like a rusty piston."

"Remember what the doctor said. It's all about exercising. That's the only way you're going to fight it." Jess knew Billy's arthritis was acting up.

"Easy for him. He's still a kid. Doesn't take him all morning to get the kinks outs. Hey, you better hurry up. You've got some tourists. You'd think they'd have something better to do than come out here on a day like this."

"What and miss my performance?"

"Yeah, you never know, there might be a talent scout from Marine World in that bunch," Billy laughed.

"Very funny. Get Kyle to help you."

"And make the kid do some honest work?"

Jess had brought Kyle Shepard onboard so that he might complete his internship from U.C. Davis. He was eager, willing, and never complained. Kyle was good to have around, and he was fond of Billy.

"Jess, I have to tell you. I'm worried about ponds three and four. This rain hasn't been good. Those back slopes are slipping down faster than a greased cat on a tin roof. I'm going to have to get the guys to fill some more sandbags."

"Let me know how it goes. And Billy...don't overdo it," Jess said.

"Can't hurt any more than I already do," Billy replied, massaging his shoulder.

Jess sprang up the step to the office.

The office was small with two desks butted together with a few file cabinets, and a long table with a copy machine, a fax machine, and a coffee maker.

Neatly framed posters hung on the walls: a blown-up photograph of a Scottish moor with an ancient castle in the background; a dramatic snapshot of a trout leaping from a brook; a serene jungle setting with fine points of light filtering down through the high branches.

Behind Jess's desk was a black-and-white poster of an emaciated child holding a small tin, staring blankly out into the room. The caption, *World Hunger Affects Us All*, was printed in bold letters beneath the child's dirty bare feet. The hatchery had joined a program that provided aide to hunger-stricken countries. Each month, the hatchery sent fish to a cannery that strictly shipped produce abroad to India and Africa.

Jess checked herself in the mirror beside the door. She made sure her ball cap with the hatchery logo was straight and her braided ponytail protruding out the back of her hat looked presentable. She was wearing a freshly pressed short-sleeved shirt also with a hatchery logo under her bomber jacket, jeans, and her favorite cowboy boots. Working outdoors, she always had a tan.

She left the office and hurried outside.

The same black sedan that had made her almost late pulled up into the parking lot.

A short, squatty man, wearing a dark suit and tie, stepped out of the car. He reached in and retrieved an attaché case. He looked around to get his bearings. Jess had no time to see what he wanted. She was already going to be late. Billy would have to attend to the jerk.

Walking around back, Jess entered a brick courtyard. A trestle overhang with interweaving ivy shaded the area.

Jess counted twelve people, mostly couples and a family grouped under the patio. One man looked over at his wife, tapping the crystal on his watch. A small boy, bundled up in his parka, was reaching into the lava rock pond, attempting to grab one of the tadpoles that quickly hid under a floating lily pad. Seeing Jess, his mother yanked him abruptly away from the pond.

"Sorry to keep you waiting," Jess said, giving everyone her tour guide smile.

"Welcome to the Murdock Fish Hatchery. My name is Jess Murdock, and I will be your guide for today."

Jess followed her script. She told them how she and her brother, Vernon, had come to work at the hatchery five years ago. After a lot of hard work, Jess had become the hatchery manager. She neglected to mention that they had inherited the business from their grandfather. The part about the hard work was true. She had busted her hump, no thanks to Vernon and his self-absorbing project that distracted him from the hatchery duties.

After a brief history of the hatchery, she touched on Vernon's work, elaborating on how she and Vernon had received their doctoral degrees from Moss Landing Marine Laboratories. As the project was confidential, she could only say that he was working on developing a new food source that would mean the end of world famine. She played it up, spurring their interest. It always tickled her to see them staring over at the Quonset hut as if the diabolical Dr. Moreau might be in there, tampering with evolution.

No one, except Vernon, was allowed inside the Quonset hut. In fact, Jess had not seen Vernon in over a month. Whatever it was that he was working on, it held him captive like a fly caught in a spider's web.

Before going inside the hatchery, Jess emphasized the importance of aquaculture, pointing out that over 14 million tons of fish were produced a year by freshwater aquaculture, contributing to fifteen percent of the world's food source. That always dazzled them.

Jess led the group into the visitor center. In one corner was a counter with a display case of T-shirts, ball caps, and pennants with the hatchery's logo for sale.

Anatomy charts and pictures of fish classifications were displayed for everyone's perusal.

One wall had an array of brown-tinted pictures of the Madison community in the early years, most of them relating one way or another to the hatchery.

Across the room on the opposite wall was the massive fish tank that always drew a gasp. Today's tour was no exception.

"That looks so natural," one woman said. "Doesn't it, Charles?"

"I'll say," Charles replied.

Jess was proud of the 500-gallon Plexiglas show tank. The backdrop resembled a riverbed, and the bottom of the tank was filled with brown gravel. Thickets of waving underwater plants undulated in the surging water driven by a jet at one end of the tank replicating the action of a flowing stream. Thirty-or-so arm-length brook trout and salmon swam against the current in suspended motion.

Jess explained the principles of fish propulsion—the caudal fin for thrust, the pectoral fin that acted as the rudder and hydroplane, the pelvic fin for controlling pitch, and the dorsal fin used for controlling roll.

Then it was off to the hatch house to see the nursery tanks. Everyone marveled at the precision of the thousands of tiny fingerlings, massing together in schools, racing in one direction, then another, keeping close ranks in clusters as if guided by a single intelligence.

Jess took the group outside to the raceways. Each raceway was ten feet wide, two hundred feet long, and eight feet deep. A narrow cement strip divided most of the raceways, but there were strips wide enough to accommodate a small crowd of people interested in peering down at the fish.

She explained how the fish were transported and stocked in nearby streams, lakes, and reservoirs around the region. Some of the trout were even sent to distributors that processed and packed the fish for supermarkets and restaurants.

They strolled past the three tanker trucks that were used to deliver the live game fish. Jess told everyone how the fish were sedated for each trip so that they did not suffer from shock and die before reaching their destination.

Nearing the end of the tour, they approached the aeration pond. Jess explained how the intake pipe from the river fed into a penstock area in the aerator pond. This provided the raceways with 700,000 gallons of fresh, oxygenated water every hour. A large fountain sprayed a huge plume above the pond.

"And these are our ponds. The ponds are used for stocking channel catfish. You might not think so, but catfish are extraordinary creatures. They have tiny bones called Weberian ossicles that connect their inner ear to their swim bladder that acts as a resonator, much like our eardrum. That's why catfish can hear four times farther than most other fish. Besides having extremely good eyesight, catfish also possess another unusual quality.

"They can taste their prey before they even see it. That's because their entire body is a taste bud, even their tail. Imagine if we could do that. Just smear a tasty treat or guilty pleasure on your skin, enjoy, wipe it off, and never gain a pound," Jess said, evoking a few chuckles from the group.

Jess spotted Kyle on a plywood platform built to cover a corner of one of the ponds. He was tossing fish food from a five-gallon bucket onto the water. Jess pointed Kyle out to everyone so that they could observe what he was doing.

"I'm sure everyone's probably heard of Pavlov, the scientist who conditioned a dog to drool each time a bell was rung signaling that it was feeding time. We've done something similar by erecting this plywood platform. The catfish have such a keen ear that they know when someone is walking above them and know it is time to be fed. By feeding them in one area, we are able to prevent overfeeding that causes bacteria in the water. And by keeping their food to one area, we are able to ensure that the fish stay healthy.

Jess felt a few drops hit the brim of her cap as it began to sprinkle.

"Looks like we just made it. I hope you all enjoyed the tour," Jess said, and waved Kyle over.

"Damn rain, when is it ever going to stop," one of the men muttered.

Kyle put the bucket down and jogged over to Jess.

"Kyle, please show these nice people out. Thanks again, folks," Jess said.

The group walked briskly back to the visitor center to get out of the rain.

Billy pulled up in the electric utility cart.

"Care for a lift?" he asked Jess.

"Not quite the stretch limo I ordered, but I guess it will do," Jess said, climbing into the cab. "Who was that guy in the black car?"

"Don't know. He wanted to see Vernon," Billy said.

"About what?"

"Didn't say exactly."

"Billy, drive up to the equipment shed and park."

"Oh, spying are we?"

"Just go."

Billy drove the cart past the ponds and parked the vehicle alongside the equipment shed. From their vantage point, they had a clear view of the only door that led into the Quonset hut.

"There they are, detective," Billy said, crouching down in his seat.

"Cut it out. They can't see us," Jess said, elbowing Billy in the ribs.

Vernon stood at the doorway. He was wearing a reddish plaid shirt, blue shorts, and knee-high black rubber boots. A brown blanket was draped over his shoulders. His hair looked as if it had never seen a comb.

"Boy, your brother needs to get out more. Who taught him how to dress? Not you, I hope."

"Oh, Billy. He looks terrible," Jess said, noting Vernon's pale complexion, wondering if her brother was suffering from anemia.

"I'm sure he's okay." Billy placed his hand on Jess's arm.

The man was talking with Vernon. Cradling his briefcase in the crook of his arm, the man opened it, and held a letter out to Vernon.

"What do you think that is?" asked Billy.

"I don't know, but it can't be good," Jess replied.

Vernon snatched the letter from the man and shoved it in the pocket of his shorts. The man began to approach Vernon, but Vernon put his hand up to ward him off.

"How has your brother been able to hold up in there for all this time? I never see him."

"He sneaks out at night. I know because I've been monitoring the ATM withdrawals on our bank statements. I'm sure you've noticed too, the missing inventory, especially chemicals. And that's not all. He even tried to secure a loan against the hatchery. The bank called me last week. Luckily, the hatchery is in both of our names. Without my signature, the bank won't process a loan."

"Damn, and all this time I thought it was my math. Vernon must be in over his head," Billy said.

"He just better not do anything stupid and jeopardize the hatchery," Jess said.

The rain started coming down in a torrential downpour. The aluminum roof of the shed sounded as though a band of crazed monkeys were beating the metal surface with drumsticks.

The man quickly closed his attaché case, held it over his head, and dashed to his car.

Vernon stood in the rain with his head tilted back letting the drops splash upon his face. He turned and went back inside.

"So what's that brother of yours up to?" asked Billy.

"I don't know," Jess replied. "But I'm starting to get a bad feeling."

CHAPTER THREE

Vernon Murdock leaned against the door in the shadowy interior of the Quonset hut. A lone incandescent light shone down on three computer monitors on a workbench.

To the left of the workbench was a cement extension of the pond, ten feet high and almost twice as wide. The left hut wall was cut two feet above ground level, allowing a view of the pond only if a person was to get down on his knees to peer out. Steel steps led up to a catwalk running along one side of the extension.

A video camera, mounted on a girder above, pointed directly into the structure. A coaxial cable ran down a beam that connected the camera to the VHS recorder on a shelf under the workbench.

Vernon shivered and stepped away from the door. He drew the blanket down around his chest. He had been so consumed in his work that he had neglected to eat properly and sleep; so it was no surprise his health had been deteriorating. At times, he wondered if he might be going crazy, cooped up and alone.

He felt a gentle breeze on the back of his neck. He turned, and saw that the door had swung open. Damn lock. He went over to the door and put his weight against it until the bolt caught in the lip of the doorjamb.

The Quonset hut had to be over fifty years old, warping and rusting into oblivion.

The rain steadily pelted the roof. The noise was almost deafening, like standing inside an echo chamber. Vernon wondered how he had been able to keep his sanity for so long.

He sloshed through the two inches of water that covered the concrete flooring.

Haphazard shafts of light shined through the roof of the building. It reminded him of the video he had rented once, *Black*

Sunday. Bruce Dern played a terrorist and had tested a prototype shrapnel bomb in a barn. After the bomb had detonated, Dern returned inside to inspect the damage. The structure of the barn had been riddled with holes. The rusting Quonset hut was in similar shape, keeping the rain out as ineffectively as a colander.

Vernon clomped up the stairs to the catwalk.

He stood at the top, bracing himself with his hands on the rail. The water down below in the channel lock that connected out to the pond was murky. The waterline mark was green with algae on the concrete walls. There was no movement in the water. It was not like them not to pay him a visit to break the monotony, anything to escape the sheer boredom of endlessly navigating the pond.

He sensed how a parent might feel, sitting by the phone waiting for a call from a son or a daughter that never came.

Disappointed, Vernon strolled back down the steps and waded over to the computer monitors. Each monitor had a number just above the screen. The number one monitor displayed data collected from various sensors positioned in the pond.

The computer evaluated the changes and growth levels of acidity, alkaline, bacteria, and algae within the pond and a bar graph in the lower left corner registered the current readings that recalculated in thirty-minute intervals. A red baseline was established for the maximum levels allowed.

Three of the bars exceeded their limits because the circulation pump had stopped working over a week ago.

Vernon had attempted to repair the pump. He'd gone out the other night and confiscated parts from the equipment shed, but after a few hours, he realized that the pump was shot. Without the pump to circulate fresh water into the pond, Zeus and Athena stood a high risk of contracting parasites that would ravage even their powerful bodies.

Normally, Vernon would also have worried about the threat of suffocation, but he knew Zeus and Athena were adaptable.

Still, he was concerned.

The second monitor displayed calculations that rapidly scrolled down the screen. The processor worked diligently to keep pace with the constant changes of Zeus and Athena. Every change exceeded the levels that Vernon had initially established. He also used this machine for documenting his research—his lifework residing on the hard drive.

The third monitor showed the tracking display. Two red blips moved sluggishly inside of a green rectangular shape. The blips were Zeus and Athena inside the pond. Vernon had tagged them with transmitters to study their swimming behavior.

Now, the transmitters held only one purpose and that was to tell Vernon whether or not Zeus and Athena were mobile, still alive.

Vernon went over to the refrigerator. The motor below rattled like the bolts and screws were about to shake loose. He opened the door and found a can of beer. Plucking the tab, Vernon took a deep swig.

Putting the beer can up to his forehead, Vernon gazed over at the fish tanks lined up on three metal tables. The tanks were arranged in a progressive order, starting with the five-gallon tanks, then ten-gallon, twenty-gallon, fifty-gallon, ending with hundred-gallon tanks. Each tank was empty, only the scum on the glass marking where the waterlines had once been.

Zeus and Athena had outgrown their homes long ago.

Vernon shuffled through the water to the unmade bed on the other end of the hut. He fell back on the mattress, resting his head on the stale-smelling pillow.

Why of all days, had they sent someone out to hound him? Couldn't they just wait? So what if they were concerned about their investment. So what if it was taking him longer that what he had predicted.

Jesus Christ! Don't you know I'm trying to save the world here?

Vernon took the crumpled envelope out of his pocket. He tore the seal and took the letter out. After a quick read, he got the jest—either show your results or repay the loan on the grant!

But what could he show them? The first two years of his work had been more of a learning process than providing results. He had the hundreds of photographs of mutated and deformed specimens to prove it. After countless disappointments, he became discouraged. Then during the third year of his research, he made a breakthrough.

That is when he began keeping his journal—*The Silurid Result*.

Steadily, he worked around the clock, sleeping only when his body demanded that he rest. By then, he had exhausted most of the grant money given to him to solve the problem of world hunger.

His goal was to develop a new aquatic species, one that would be a prime food source for the world to share.

But as each year progressed, Vernon's experiments soon strayed from their intended path, and eventually, Zeus and Athena evolved.

Vernon glanced at his watch, too exhausted to think straight.

It was almost noon, and he already had the chills and the sweats.

His eyes burned from lack of sleep, and his body was completely drained of energy. He closed his eyes and drifted off into a deep sleep.

The nightmare was basically the same with slight variations. Vernon would be wrapped in a bed of kelp, or tangled in a mass of hoses, or having the life squeezed out of him by enormous tentacles.

And the water would teem with his blood.

CHAPTER FOUR

Nell's brother thought it would be funny and cranked the wheel in the direction of the cat dashing across the road.

"Stop it, Sean!" Nell yelled, slugging him in the arm.

Sean ignored her and made the golf cart go even faster.

"Sean!"

The cat—seeing its nine lives flash before its eyes—screeched in alarm.

Sean veered away and not a second too soon, almost clipping the animal.

"Don't get so excited, I wasn't going to hit it," he laughed.

Nell caught a glimpse of the terrified cat darting into the rain. She could never understand why Sean got such a kick out of tormenting her and never missed an opportunity to scare her.

"Yeah, you were, you dope!"

"Watch out or I'll make you walk."

"You do and I'll tell Mom."

"Yeah, you would you little tattletale."

"I'm no tattletale," Nell said.

Never willing to cut her any slack, Sean steered the golf cart into a large puddle.

Muddy water splashed everywhere. Luckily, they were in their raingear. Both Sean's poncho and Nell's yellow slicker were splattered with mud, but it was Max sitting in the rear cargo bed that got the brunt of it. He stood up and shook off, getting Sean back by flicking gobs of mud back at him.

"That'll teach you," Nell giggled.

"You laugh now," Sean said, wiping mud off his cheek.

They stopped at a set of steps leading up to a deck outside a trailer.

Nell jumped from the golf cart.

"I'll be back in an hour to pick you up. You better be ready," Sean said, and sped off.

Nell ran up the stairs to the porch. She used her secret code, two knocks, a pause, then three more knocks on the screen door.

The hinges creaked as the door slowly opened.

"Well, if isn't my favorite little scholar. Prompt as always," said Professor Jonathan Stone, holding open the door.

"Does that mean I get a star, Professor?" Nell asked, stepping inside.

"Absolutely."

Nell took off her rain slicker and hung it on a hook by the door to dry. She sat on a short stool and removed her galoshes and set them by the door. Walking in her stocking feet, she glanced in the kitchen.

Today, she only saw a few dishes in the sink. Professor Stone was far from being a clean freak. Chunks of chopped white meat were piled on a cutting board left on the messy kitchen table covered with fish guts and bloodstained newspaper—carp, courtesy of Sean.

Professor Stone was waiting for her in the living room. He pulled a book from a shelf, thumbed through the contents, then placed a bookmark inside and closed the book.

"Would you mind tending to our friends while I look for a video for today's session?" he asked and left the room.

"Sure," Nell said.

Professor Stone's living room was unlike any other. Sure, he had his favorite chair, a TV stand with a VCR, a small table, and a couch, but that was pretty much it for furniture.

The rest of the room was occupied by bookshelves crammed with more books than what were in the Madison Library and more aquariums than could be found in a small pet store.

Nell went over to her favorite aquarium.

Three red-tailed sharks—she had fondly named them Huey, Dewey, and Louie—swam together like the best of friends. Their bodies were black except for their tails, which were bright red. Though they looked like four-inch long sharks, Professor Stone said they were really members of the carp family.

She sprinkled some fish food on the surface.

Last session, she had learned the importance of a fish's swim bladder. The swim bladder would fill with gas and kept the fish from sinking to the bottom. If a fish did not have a fish bladder, it had to keep swimming so that oxygen would flow through its gills.

The *real* sharks in the sea did not have swim bladders, so they had to keep swimming all the time. That meant they never slept. Nell knew how cranky she could get whenever she missed her nap. She guessed that was why sharks were always so mean and ate people.

Her second favorite aquarium was the one with the clown loaches.

They were yellow mostly with black stripes. Slightly longer than the red-tailed sharks, the ten fish swam vertically rather than horizontally. One clown loach was on the bottom of the tank, lying on its side. Any other fish, and Nell would have been yelling for Professor Stone to tell him one of his fish had died. She knew better, having already fallen for their pranks.

The clown loach was only resting, playing a trick on her.

Nell could hear Professor Stone in the spare bedroom still searching for the tape he had promised. She crossed the room to the other aquariums.

In one of the tanks was a slinky-looking fish with whiskers sticking out around its mouth. She had nicknamed the fish— Zapper. The fish was gray with flecked spots. All of Zapper's fins were near its tail.

She watched a curious goldfish—a feeder—swim too close to the electric catfish. The goldfish jerked, stunned, and sank to the bottom.

Zapper swooped down and gobbled up his paralyzed prey.

Nell knew better than to pet this *cat*. She gave Zapper a disgusted look and went over to another aquarium.

Of all the aquariums, she disliked this one the most but was always drawn to the glass. It was like being in the car and glancing out the window and seeing something dead on the side of the road.

As gross as it might be, you were still compelled to look.

That's how she felt whenever she looked inside this tank. The fish were definitely strange. They had heads for bodies and jagged little teeth. Their bodies were speckled with yellow and green glitter. She had never felt an attachment so she never named them.

Most of the time, they barely moved. They would just stare, motionless, almost like they weren't even alive.

Hey, little girl. How about reaching in and giving us a pet?

They gave her the creeps.

Strange, the last time she had looked in this aquarium, there had been six piranhas.

Now there were only five. Perhaps they had grown tired of being fed the scraps of carp and needed something tastier, even if it was one of their own.

"I thought I'd never find it," Professor Stone said, coming back into the room.

"Is it a National Geographic?" Nell asked. She took a seat on the couch.

"I believe so, yes." He inserted the tape into the VCR and turned on the TV.

A desert scene appeared on the television screen. The colors were faded and seemed to blend together.

"I taped this off PBS years ago. It's a little grainy, but I think you will enjoy it."

The narrator told a story about the desert and how animals coped with the heat.

Nell watched different types of animals drinking from various watering holes.

Professor Stone picked up the remote control and fast-forwarded the tape. A zebra struggled to free itself from thick mud in fast motion.

The image changed and was slowed down to normal speed, showing brightly colored fish floating in a pond, blowing bubbles to the surface.

"Those are Japanese fighting fish called Betas. See those bubbles they are making? That's where they keep their eggs."

"That's weird," Nell said.

"Wait till you see this," Professor Stone said.

The camera zoomed in on an extreme close-up of the inside of a fish's mouth.

"There are some species of fish that protect their young by housing them in their mouth."

"That's gross," Nell said, and made a face when she saw the fish's mouth packed with roe.

"That's so other fish won't eat her babies."

Another segment showed a fish crawling out of a mud hole.

"See that, Nell. That is what's called a *walking* catfish. The scientific name is *Clarias batrachus.* It can actually breathe out of water. Watch."

Nell stared at the screen and watched the fish wiggle its way out of the mud then used its fins to crawl over to another water hole.

"Can the catfish in the lake do that?"

"No. The fish you see here has adapted to its surrounding. In order for it to survive, it must be able to migrate to a new water source. This catfish actually has lung-like organs, much like ours. Pretty remarkable, wouldn't you say?"

"Wow, I could put it on a leash and take it for a walk," Nell laughed.

The picture on the television turned blue, signaling that the tape was over.

There was a knock on the front door.

"Is that Sean already?" Nell said, realizing that her hour was up.

Professor Stone glanced at his wristwatch.

"See how time flies when you're having fun." He smiled. "Grab your gear, and I'll see you tomorrow."

Nell jumped off the couch and ran to the front door. She threw on her slicker and slipped her boots on.

"Bye-bye," she said and raced out the door.

It was drizzling when she came outside but not raining as hard as before. She made sure not to slip on the steps and hopped into the awaiting golf cart.

"Before we go home, Devon wants me to check the Pumpkin Eater and make sure she's not taking on water," Sean said.

The rain was in their faces, so Sean didn't drive as fast and reckless as earlier.

Nell was glad.

Sean was a daredevil and loved scaring her, but he wasn't mean-spirited.

Devon always got on Sean's case, said he wasn't responsible and that sometimes he acted like a kid much younger than his age and that it was time to grow up. Without their father around to watch over them, Devon was often forced to assume the parental role.

They soon reached the cove below their trailer and stopped on the beach.

Wooden steps led up the embankment to the McNeeley's patio.

"Go ahead, I'll be up in a second," Sean said.

Nell ran toward the steps. She had a ritual she always did every time she went up or down the steps. Going down, she counted each step from one to twenty-two. Going up, she counted backward.

"Twenty-two, twenty-one, twenty—" Nell said aloud. She counted the rest to herself and raced up to the porch.

***

Kate stood in the kitchen of her mobile home and was buttering the last cob of corn. She seasoned it with black pepper, rolled it in aluminum foil, and placed it on a foiled stack occupying a platter.

"Where did I put my wine?" Kate said, scouting around the cluttered kitchen.

"Behind you, on the counter," Kelly replied. She tossed some tomatoes slices into a salad bowl.

"So it is." Kate picked up the glass and polished it off. She poured herself another glass. She could smell the delicious aromas of crayfish steaming in garlic and the barbeque wafting through the open kitchen window.

"Hmmm." She took a deep breath and leaned against the counter sipping her wine.

Once a week, Kate threw a barbeque for the neighbors. It was her way of showing her appreciation, an excuse to have an evening when she did not allow herself to fret about the resort.

"This is a new look. What do you call it?" Kate asked, brushing Kelly's blue hair back from her face while the teenager chopped up stalks of celery.

"Boysenberry. You like it?"

"It's different. Think that color would suit me?"

"Yeah, right. Next, you'll be telling me you want to get a body piercing," Kelly said, shaking her head.

"Well, I had considered getting a diamond stud for my nose."

"I'm sure," Kelly said.

"Really. But then I decided against it. I was too afraid of sneezing one day and putting someone's eye out."

"Like you would do that."

"Yeah, that's silly. But a key chain wouldn't be a bad idea," Kate said, scrunching her eyebrows while pondering the thought.

"No, think about it. You know how I'm always misplacing my keys. I would never have to worry about them again. They would always be right there under my nose."

Kate burst out laughing.

"You had me going there for a second," Kelly said, busting up.

"We better set the table," Kate said, grabbing the platter of wrapped corn.

"I'll get the cutlery," Kelly said.

Kate pushed the door open and went out onto the deck.

The party was just getting started despite the rain. Everyone stayed dry under the patio cover.

Jasper pulled on a Corona and watched Sean stir the pot of crawdads cooking on a Coleman stove.

Jasper leaned over the pot to get a whiff.

"Watch out, Mr. Joyner. You get a hair in there, everyone's going to blame me," Sean said.

"It isn't stew, boy," Jasper said, but stood back anyway.

Claude was sitting at the table, munching on tortilla chips. He grabbed a chip from the bowl, dipped it in a plastic container, and shoved the chip in his mouth.

"Devon, honey, here's the corn." Kate passed Devon the platter. He lifted the lid on the propane barbeque. Pork spareribs were cooking on the bottom rack of the grill. He dumped the foiled corn on the top rack and arranged them in orderly rows with a pair of tongs.

The trout Claude had caught that morning were cooking to a golden brown on the second rack.

Max sat next to Devon, hoping that something might slide off the grill.

Kelly came out with a plastic container full of forks, knives, and spoons. Nell was right behind her carrying a package of napkins. They began setting the table.

"When's this rain ever going to let up," Kate said, easing down in a chaise lounge next to Liz Fallow. Rosie was asleep on the deck near Liz's feet.

Rain drizzled off the lip of the patio cover.

"It's enough to depress the hell out of anyone," Liz said, bitterly.

"Thank God, El Nino wasn't around in biblical times or Noah would still be adrift."

"Kate, you amaze me."

"Oh?"

"How do you keep your spirits up?"

"I'll admit things could be better, but there's no point on dwelling on it. You learn to take the bad with the good," Kate said.

"You are something, raising these kids on your own, running this place. I have to hand it to you, Kate."

"Thanks, Liz. That means a lot."

"I don't want you to get angry, but I have to ask."

"This isn't about Max and Rosie again, is it?"

"I'm afraid so."

"Max, have you been a bad boy?"

As soon as Max heard his name, he sauntered over next to Kate and sat by her side. Kate kneaded Max's scruff while she talked with Liz.

"Whenever I let Rosie out to do her business, she runs off with Max."

"Well, dogs will be dogs. Isn't that right, boy?" Max leaned into Kate's hand.

"But Rosie always comes back looking such a fright and smelling something terrible. I hate to think what they get into. Is there any way you could restrain Max?"

"Pen him up? I couldn't do that. He needs to roam, don't you, boy? If he doesn't have the run of the place, he just becomes a pest with his barking and whining," Kate said.

"I thought you might say that."

"I wouldn't worry. Hey, maybe some day Max and Rosie will—"

"Kate! Bite your tongue!" Liz's loud outburst woke up Rosie. The dog looked around in a panic as though a firecracker had suddenly gone off.

Max trotted over and licked Rosie's face to console her.

"Max, you're such the lover," Kate said.

Once Professor Stone arrived, they all sat down to dinner. Kate, Kelly, Devon, and Sean sat on one side of the long table while the professor, Claude, Jasper, and Nell sat on the other side. Max and Rosie were under the table nestled between everyone's feet.

The gloom of night slowly crept in, stealing away the view of the lake. A string of Tiki lights illuminated the patio.

The rain came down steadily while they ate dinner.

"I'd like to make a toast," Claude said, raising his glass of wine.

Everyone set their knives and forks down, lifted their glasses.

"To great friends and food to boot," Claude said with a toothy grin.

"Yeah, it doesn't get any better than this," Jasper chimed in.

"I'll second that," Kate said.

"Let's not forget the lake," Professor Stone said. "You've got to admit, Lake Recluse does stand up to its name. I don't think you could find a more peaceful place." He reached over and clinked his glass against Kate's.

"Boring is more like it," Sean piped in.

"Maybe I'm not giving you enough to do around here, if you're bored," Devon said.

"How do you figure? You work me like a dog."

"Yeah, and when we aren't working, we got our noses stuck in a book," Nell said.

"Do I detect a little rebellion brewing?" Kate discerned.

"When is the last time we had some fun?" Sean asked.

"Well, the resort doesn't run itself."

"Who cares," Sean said, glaring down at his plate.

"Why don't you all go tubing tomorrow?" Kate said. She knew being cooped up and the dreary weather was giving her family a touch of cabin fever. Going out on the lake would be a nice diversion for Sean and Nell.

"Mom, the lake is freezing this time of year," Devon protested.

"Wear your wetsuits. Just make sure Nell keeps warm."

"You're serious?"

"All right!" Sean shouted. "Can I be excused? *Seinfeld* is almost on."

"Take your plate in," Kate said.

Sean grabbed his plate and ran inside.

"Can I be excused, too?" Nell asked.

"Yes, you may."

"I want to get an early start in the morning, so I think I'll be pushing off," Claude said.

"Me, too. Hate to eat and run," Jasper said.

"Kate, that was a great meal. But I must confess, I didn't care much for the cheese dip," Claude said.

"Cheese dip? Claude, we only put out salsa," Kate said.

"So that's where I left my bait. I was looking all over for that," Jasper said, picking up the plastic container and snapping the lid back on.

"What? Are you trying to poison me? You did that on purpose," Claude said.

"Hey, if you're stupid enough to eat it."

Jasper took off running. For being a big man, he could still make a hasty retreat especially when Claude was hot on his heels. Jasper fled down the steps and jumped in his golf cart and sped down the road.

"Night, Kate," Claude hollered back over his shoulder.

"Those two are worse than a couple of kids," Kate said.

"Let me help you with the dishes," Professor Stone said, picking up his plate.

"You just sit and relax, Jonathan. We'll clean up. There's a bottle of scotch in that cooler," Kate said, pointing to the icebox next to one of the chaise lounges.

"You will be out soon to join me, won't you?" asked Professor Stone.

"Make mine a double," Kate replied. Kelly and Liz helped with clearing off the table and they went inside.

"Would you like to join me?" Professor Stone asked Devon.

"I better not. I should go down to the marina and check the boats." Devon waved and scurried down the steps to his golf cart.

Professor Stone reached inside the cooler. He took out the bottle of scotch and a plastic cup, added some ice, and poured. He put the bottle back in the cooler and sat down on a chaise lounge. He held his drink on his lap and gazed out onto the moonlit lake.

He glanced down and saw Max and Rose fast asleep together on the deck.

It's true what Jasper said. It doesn't get any better than this!

The professor sipped his drink.

Crickets chirped in the night. He had read somewhere that crickets could predict the temperature. If a person counted the amount of times a cricket chirped in fifteen seconds then added forty, the total would equal the present temperature in degrees Fahrenheit.

The professor was diligently listening to a nearby cricket when Kate came out and sat down in the chaise lounge next to him.

Kelly and Liz stepped out of the mobile home. "Thank you for dinner. It was delightful," Liz said, slapping her thigh for Rosie to follow.

"I put Nell to bed. She fell asleep on the couch. Sean is still glued to the tube," Kelly said. She came over and gave Kate a hug.

"Stay safe in this rain," Kate said.

Kelly and Liz waved goodbye and left.

Professor Stone poured Kate a drink and handed it to her.

"Thanks." She held the cup on her lap and stared out at the lake.

The professor consulted his wristwatch, made a mental calculation, and looked over at the temperature gauge hanging on a patio post. The gauge read sixty-five degrees, same as the cricket's prediction. He laughed out loud.

"What's so funny?" Kate asked.

"Oh, nothing," he smiled.

All the millions spent on meteorology when a damn bug could do the job!

CHAPTER FIVE

"We need more sandbags down here," Billy yelled over the deafening rain. Two halogen lamps were mounted on stands shining down on the foreman. He was standing in the gully with his boots submerged clear up to his shins in the mud at the base of the embankment of one of the ponds.

"Gus, speed it up," Jess said.

"Going as fast as I can," Gus said. He was working under a rain repellent canopy, filling sandbags with a shovel. An unlit soggy cigar poked out of the corner of his mouth.

Gus Fern was one of Billy's crew. Gus was strong as an ox and paced himself with the same temperament.

"This is hopeless," Jess said, staring down at the base of the pond fifteen feet below.

Billy and Kyle were down in the gully, doing their best to fortify the eroding hillside, but their efforts seemed to be in vain. The muddy runoff kept seeping out through the ineffective sandbags like jam squeezing out the crusts of a P&J sandwich.

"You two better get up here! We're just going to have to wait until the rain lets up," Jess yelled.

"We're on our way," Billy said, motioning for Kyle to climb up first. Kyle reached for a secure handhold and dug the toes of his boots into the sandbags. Billy waited until Kyle was halfway up before beginning his ascent. He followed Kyle's route like a trusting mountain climber scaling a precipice.

Jess watched them struggle up the wall of shifting sandbags. Gus joined her, leaning down with his hands on his knees to get a better look.

"You better hurry. This hill is not going to hold for much longer," Gus said.

Kyle was reaching for the next sandbag when it suddenly came down. Unable to brace himself, he fell backward. An avalanche of sandbags slid down after him.

Kyle landed on his back, the thick mud and sandbags breaking some of the fall.

"Kyle, are you okay?" Jess yelled.

"Yeah, I'll live." Kyle struggled to sit up.

Jess could hear the mud sucking at his clothes as he tried to scramble to his feet.

"Where's Billy?" she shouted.

"He's trapped under the sandbags!"

***

Less than a mile away, Bud Warner, a hydrologist with the U.S. Geological Survey, was standing on the Madison Levee. The heavy rain blurred most of his view of the nearby hatchery. He could just make out the Quonset hut and the cinder block wall beyond the field. He had to strain to see the rooftops and steeples of Madison.

He shined his flashlight out on the Sacramento River. He had never seen the river so turbulent and swollen. The current was strong and fast enough to create white caps on the rippling waves sweeping by. Tree limbs and debris passed like hitchhikers stealing a ride.

He redirected the beam of the flashlight to the single lane asphalt road on the crest of the levee. The service road had been paved a few years after the levee had been constructed, but was too difficult to maintain. Caltrans later engineered the frontage road.

Bud proceeded down the road checking for structural damage. He shivered, the chilling wind cutting through his jacket.

What the hell am I doing up here? I could be home with a tall one, catching the game.

He reached into his pocket, pulled out his cellular phone. He held the flashlight so he could see the push buttons. He kept walking, pressing the buttons with his thumb.

Bud was about to make the connection when he looked down at his feet.

The road was gone.

"Damn," he said, stepping back. The asphalt broke off just where he was about to place his next step. He shined his light across the crevice. It was more than ten feet wide. Water was seeping through the thin wall that separated the river from the other side of the levee. Large clumps of mud toppled down onto the frontage road.

Bud dialed his phone. He had to warn the town. The levee was breaking up. He looked over at the distant hatchery and prayed there was no one there.

***

Gus tied a rope to a fence post then tossed the end down to Kyle. Jess drew a slack portion of rope behind her waist and rappelled down the hill.

"Where did you last see him?" Jess asked, not sure where to start their search for Billy. There were over fifty sandbags piled up in the gully.

"Ah jeez, judging where I landed, he must be under here somewhere," Kyle said.

"Don't worry, Kyle. We'll find him," Jess said, lifting up a sandbag.

"Billy! Billy, can you hear me?" Kyle yelled. He began dragging off the top sandbags.

Gus made it down without disturbing the sandbags still meshed into the hillside.

"Don't worry old man, we'll get you out of there," Gus said. He lifted a forty-pound sandbag and flung it in the air like it was only a five-pound bag of sugar. He grabbed another sandbag and tossed that one even further.

Jess heard a faint moan.

"He's under here," she said, pointing.

Gus and Kyle got down on their knees and pulled back the sandbags.

Jess could see Billy's mud-smeared face. He was grinning like a kid with a mouthful of chocolate.

"Took you long enough," he said. "If I wanted a mud bath, I would have gone to Calistoga. Mind helping me out of here?"

Billy showed no signs of being injured except for his pride and the indignation of being buried in the mud.

A siren began to wail from the direction of Madison.

"What's that?" Jess said. "I've never heard that before."

"This isn't good," Gus said.

"What isn't?" Kyle asked.

"It's the flood alarm."

"Hey, what the—?" Flowing water swept over Billy's face. He gurgled to catch a breath.

"Get him out of there, hurry!" Jess yelled, reaching down to pull Billy's head above the water.

They could hear a flood of water coming their way.

"The levee must have broke!" Gus grabbed two sandbags and tossed them to the side.

"He's free," Kyle said, pulling Billy up by the arms.

The water steadily rose in the gully until they were standing waist-deep.

"Gus, help Billy up," Jess said.

Gus threw Billy over his shoulder and began climbing the rope.

"Come on, Kyle, you're next."

"Ladies first," Kyle said.

"This is no time to fool around. If you haven't noticed, we're standing on low ground. Move it!"

Kyle grabbed the rope and scampered up the sandbags.

Jess waited until Kyle was halfway up then grabbed the wet rope and began her ascent. She heard a rumble, a sudden surge of floodwater.

"Kyle, hurry!" Jess screamed.

A hand snared Jess's arm and yanked her up. Gus had come to her rescue.

An enormous wave crashed along the outside slopes of the ponds.

Safe for the moment on top of the embankment, Jess knelt over Billy.

"Billy, are you okay?"

"Yeah, I'm fine," he said, and slowly got to his feet.

"Jess, you better take a look," Gus said, pointing toward the Quonset hut.

"Oh, my God," she said. The floodwater had undermined the foundation of the cinder block wall, causing it to collapse. The backsides of two ponds were completely washed away, releasing the catfish into the flash flood waters rushing down the gully.

Hundreds of catfish leaped in the moonlight. Jess had never seen such a spectacular sight.

"I need to go change," Billy said, covered in mud.

"Yeah, we need a break out of this rain," Jess said.

"I'm for that," Kyle said.

"You guys go ahead. I'm going to check the pumps on the raceways," Gus said and trudged off in the pouring rain.

***

Vernon woke up to the smell of smoke. The acrid stench made his eyes water and smelt like burning plastic. He shot up from bed and ran over to the workbench.

All three monitors and processors were sputtering sparks and engulfed in flames.

He grabbed a fire extinguisher, pulled the pin, and discharged a smothering spray of powder onto the fire. Once it was all out, he stood and stared, his research reduced to a black, gooey mess.

Something told him to go up to the catwalk. Once there, his fears were confirmed. The concrete extension from the pond was empty.

He raced down the steps to the workbench. The VHS tapes that he had recorded all of his research were ruined, floating in one of the drawers. In a fit of temper, he ripped a few drawers out of their slides and hurled them across the flooded floor.

He fell to his knees and pounded the water with his fists. He looked up and was able to see out below the Quonset hut wall.

There was only darkness beyond the pond. The cinder block wall had collapsed, and the water in the pond had drained out.

Zeus and Athena were gone!

"NOOO!" he screamed at the top of his lungs.

Vernon stood and went over to one of the drawers still in the workbench. He took out a topography map and unfolded it. He hunched over the map, drawing lines with a marker pen.

"There's only one place for you to go," he said, and circled a spot on the map.

He left the map on the workbench and began collecting what was salvageable.

Vernon made a few trips out to his truck: some dry clothes, camping gear, an inflatable four-man raft with a wooden transom, an outboard motor and gas tank, a portable pump, and a mobile tracking device.

He climbed into the cab, started up the truck, and sped off into the night.

***

"I tell you, it was weird. I was checking the pumps when I heard this ungodly cry coming from the Quonset hut. It was Vernon. And then I saw him packing up his truck. Then he took off like a bat out of hell," Gus said, relaying what he had seen while they walked toward the Quonset hut.

"That is strange," Jess said. Billy and Kyle were walking alongside, shaking their heads, just as bewildered.

They were just approaching the entrance when a gust of wind blew across their backs, and the door swung open.

The four entered the building, shining their lights in every direction.

"Smells like there was a fire in here," Kyle said, wading toward the workbench.

Gus slogged through the water to the rear of the building.

"What do you make of this?" Billy asked, shining his light on the concrete wall.

"Let's take a look," Jess said, and they climbed the steps to the catwalk.

They stood on the catwalk and shined their light down into the algae-covered extension of the pond.

"Must have been a good twenty feet deep when it was full, judging by the waterline," Billy said.

"Check out those markings," Jess said, shining her light on the top lip of the wall. "There are two distinct measurements. Each one is identified with an *A* and a *Z*. I wonder what they mean? By the dates, they look like growth charts. Reminds me of when we used to get our heights notched on the doorjamb when we were kids."

"That's impossible. Those markings are nearly thirty feet long," Billy said.

"Hey, look what I found," Kyle shouted.

Jess and Billy came down to see what Kyle had discovered.

"Vernon marked up this map. Might show us where he went?"

Billy looked down at the map. "That's Adobe Creek. Just behind the hatchery."

"He's circled something here," Kyle said.

"That's Lake Recluse," Jess said, feeling a knot form in her stomach.

"Over here," Kyle shouted. "Check this stuff out." He had wandered over to the drawers that had been yanked from the workbench and thrown about the place.

They waded over to where Kyle stood and began inspecting the drawers.

"Looks like Vernon kept some sort of journal. It's a little soggy," Kyle said.

"Can I have that?" Jess asked. She took the book from Kyle and read the cover: *The Silurid Result*. "I better keep this."

"There's a bunch of tapes here, but I'm afraid they won't be much use to us," Billy said, holding up a dripping wet VHS tape.

"Too bad they all got damaged," Gus said.

Kyle scooted under the hanging wall that led outside to the pond.

"So are we any closer to knowing what Vernon was doing in here?" Billy asked.

"I'm still not sure," Jess said.

"You guys better get out here," Kyle called from outside.

"What's he found now?" Billy asked.

They stooped under the hanging wall and joined Kyle, standing on the edge of the empty pond.

"Shine your lights down there," Kyle said.

Everyone directed the beams of their flashlights on the muddy bottom of the large pond.

"Holy shit!" Gus said.

"Dear God," Jess said.

"I guess now we know," Billy said.

They stood silently and gawked at the two deep behemoth impressions in the mud that stretched half the length of the pond like a pair of intact prehistoric fossils.

***

For hours, the raging waters flowed through the ruptured levee and raced down the gullied stretch known as Adobe Creek. After a forty-mile journey, the overflowing creek surged into Lake Recluse.

A coyote howled in the hills above the remote shoreline. Nocturnal creatures rustled in the underbrush. The predators sensed the urgency in their quest, as it was only an hour before sunrise.

The moon poked its face out of the rain-spent clouds, the night sky and mountains reflected on the lake's surface.

A gaggle of Canadian geese flew down for a rest stop. Breaking their perfect V-formation, the birds tilted back their wings and made their approach. Their webbed feet slowed their descent, skidding onto the water.

There was a ruction of honks and splashing while the geese reveled in the brief time allotted before continuing on their journey. The weary travelers floated aimlessly, dipping their long necks into the water, searching for fish.

Suddenly, the geese began to panic, rustling their wings. Some of them attempted to take flight, but couldn't seem to get off the water. They honked in desperation, shuddering, until all thirty birds floated dead on the water.

Before a wisp of cloud could slash the face of the moon, the birds were sucked under.

CHAPTER SIX

Jasper lugged his fishing gear down the hill. For some reason, the bank on this side of Chickaree Creek looked different. It took him awhile before he realized that the creek was wider. Must be from all the rain. That was okay, the deeper the water, the bigger the fish.

He quickly set up on the new bank in the early morning sun.

He opened his lawn chair a foot away from the water, placed his cooler to the right and his tackle box to the left for easy access, giving him no reason to have to get out of his chair. He pushed the pole holders in the sand and stuck in his two fishing rods. He loved the new fishing regulation allowing a fisherman to use two poles, as long as he stayed within a certain distance of the rigs. There was enough beer in the cooler to last him the day.

He baited his 1/0 hooks with Berkley Power Bait, ensuring that the tips of the hooks and the barbs were hidden inside the yellow gob that looked more like Play-Doh than fish bait.

Jasper picked up his first pole and opened the bail. He let the line lay across the crook of his finger and tested the weight of the slip shot. He brought the rod back and whipped it forward in the direction of the middle of the stream. The end of his line dropped exactly where he wanted it. He reeled in the slack, sticking the pole in the holder. He quickly baited up the second rod and cast the line out.

Rather than have to stare at his poles waiting for a strike, Jasper clipped small bells on the tips of each pole. A nibble or a bite, and the bells would ring.

Jasper reached into his cooler, grabbed a can of beer, and popped the tab. He was about to take a gulp when one of the bells shook. The tip of the pole dipped, almost touching the water.

"Hot damn!" He grabbed the rod and began reeling in the line.

The fish broke the surface. It was a fat two-pound catfish.

He brought the fish ashore and reached down to remove the hook.

The fish thrashed to get back into the water.

"No, you don't," he said, holding the wriggling fish down with his boot. The last thing he wanted was to get poked by one of those sharp spines that were on each side of its mouth. He'd been jabbed before and remembered how his hand had swollen up from the nasty venom.

He had just fed the fish onto a stringer when the other bell began to ring. This time, the pole was almost yanked out of the holder.

"This must be my lucky day!" He reeled in another catfish, this one bigger than the one before.

He wasted no time, baited the hooks, and cast out. Before he could even reach for his beer, the bells started ringing, both at the same time.

Good Lord, I must have died and gone to fisherman's heaven!

Again, they were catfish. He set them on the stringer and decided to take a short beer break. He kicked back in his chair and looked upstream.

Claude was standing on the shore, about seventy feet away.

"Hey, Claude. What do you think of these beauties?" Jasper gloated, raising the stringer of fish.

Claude flipped him the finger.

"What's that? Your IQ or your sperm count?" Jasper laughed. He knew Claude was still sore about the cheese dip stunt from the barbeque.

He took a gulp of his beer and thought he would watch Claude before resuming fishing. There was no hurry. For some unfathomable reason, the stream was miraculously teeming with fish.

Claude stepped into his chest waders. Carrying his fly rod, he stepped out into the shallows and began casting, forward and backward. He played out more line with each forward cast. He was paying too much attention placing his fly, neglecting what was behind him, and ended up backward casting his line and tangling it in a low-hanging branch.

"Swift move," Jasper yelled, laughing so hard he almost fell out of his lawn chair.

Claude tugged at the line, but the filament was wound tight around the branch. He gave it a hard yank and broke the branch off. The tree limb fell, landing in the water, and slowly floated downstream.

"Oh, you're killing me," Jasper howled. This time, he pitched out of his chair.

"Bite me, Jasper," Claude yelled. He shoved his reel inside the strap of his suspenders. He took his pipe out of his shirt pocket and fumbled for a match.

A pair of meadowlarks swept down and perched on the floating branch.

Jasper sat up in the sand, tears rolling down his cheeks. "Looks like you caught something after all!" He was laughing so hard he thought he would pee his pants.

He chuckled to himself and got up, baited a hook, and cast out his line. He leaned down to shove the handle of his rod into the pole holder.

A foot-high swell washed ashore right over his boots.

"What the—?" He looked for the cause and saw something strange out on the water.

It was too big to be a log. A sandbar perhaps, but that didn't make sense. He had fished this same spot a hundred times and never remembered a sandbar in the middle of the creek. And why would a sandbar suddenly appear out of nowhere when the creek level was so high?

He shielded his eyes from the morning sun to get a better look at the elliptic-shaped mass fifty feet away. His first assumption had been wrong. It wasn't made of sand. It looked more like shale stepping-stones all bunched together.

And it wasn't stationary. It was moving.

Drifting upstream.

Coming straight for Claude.

"What do you make of that?" Jasper yelled, looking over at Claude.

Claude was fussing with his pipe, purposely ignoring Jasper.

Jasper glanced back at the water and caught a glimpse of the two meadowlarks perched on the floating branch—just before they were sucked under.

"Jesus, Claude! Did you see that?"

Claude lit his pipe and was about to flick the match when the line at the end of his fly rod went taut and he was pulled forward. He made a futile attempt to unhook the reel from his suspender.

He was yanked in face-first, the water rushing into the front of his chest waders.

Jasper watched Claude go under.

"Claude!" Jasper reached in his tackle box and grabbed his fillet knife. His plan was to go in the water, intercept Claude, and cut the filament setting him free.

He was about to enter the water when he heard a strange crackling sound. He looked down and saw a dozen or more catfish floating on the surface.

They looked dead.

He reached down and put his hand in the water to touch the nearest fish.

"Damn," he yelled when he was jolted backward, landing hard on his butt.

Somehow, he had just gotten shocked.

His skin felt tingly, just like the time he had forgotten to throw the circuit breaker and nearly electrocuted himself trying to fix a fool light switch.

"Jasper, help—" Claude yelled, coming up for air.

Jasper watched Claude drift by. What could he do? He felt helpless. Sure, Claude was a pain in the ass, and they were always on each other's case, but he was the closest thing to a friend Jasper ever knew.

He looked downstream. A tree had uprooted from the storm and fallen partly across the creek. If he hurried, he might be able to snare Claude, cut him loose.

Jasper took off running. Even he was surprised how fast he could move when he wanted to. Not that he would break any Olympic records. When he reached the fallen tree, he didn't even think twice, just jumped up, and started shuffling out over the creek.

You've only one chance, Buddy Boy, so you better make it good!

He got down on his knees, grabbed a branch, and leaned out.

Claude came within arm's reach and held onto the log.

Jasper sliced through the suspender.

Claude's $400 fly rod and reel disappeared downstream.

"Try and pull yourself up!"

"I'm trying!" Claude's chest waders were completely filled with water. It was like having an anchor wrapped around his legs.

"Hook onto my belt! I'm going to cut the other suspender!"

Jasper cut the fabric. Claude paddled and kicked his legs. The heavy chest waders slipped down past his waist, and after more struggling, Claude was finally able to squirm out of them.

Jasper helped Claude clamber onto the fallen tree trunk.

"I never thought I would be saying this—thanks."

"Couldn't let you drown," Jasper said, smirking. "You're too much fun to have around."

"What the hell just happened?" Claude asked.

Jasper looked out over the creek.

The sandbar, or whatever the damn thing was, was gone.

"I have no idea."

"Me neither."

Jasper and Claude sat on the fallen log, dangling their feet over the water like a couple of misfits out of a Mark Twain novel.

CHAPTER SEVEN

"Are you sure you don't want me to tag along?" Billy asked.

"No, I'll be okay. Besides, I need you here to run things," Jess replied.

Jess climbed into the Bronco and started the engine.

"Hey, wait a minute," Billy said. He ran up the steps and darted into the office. He came back out carrying a satchel. He went around to the passenger side and pulled on the handle, but the door would not open.

"Unlock the door," he said.

"It is unlocked. The stupid thing keeps sticking." Jess leaned across the console and pushed the door. The door creaked open.

"Here, you don't want to forget this," Billy said, and put the satchel on the passenger seat.

"Thanks, Billy."

"You be careful."

"I will. Don't worry."

Billy closed the door and waved goodbye.

***

Jess had been driving on the interstate for forty-five minutes when she happened to glance at the digital clock on the dashboard. The time was 7:38. It was good that Billy had remembered the satchel. Inside was Vernon's journal, which was of grave importance to her brother.

A highway sign came into view: Route 7. Blue placards hung beneath with icons of a boat and a gas pump.

She took the exit looping to an underpass and turned left at the Lake Recluse 37 miles sign.

For thirty minutes, she drove the windy road that weaved up into the hills. It was a slow drive, especially with the hairpin turns forcing her to reduce her speed down to 20 miles an hour. Not a drive that she would cherish having to do every day. She saw black skid marks at one bend where a driver had slammed on the brakes either going too fast or attempting to avoid hitting an animal in the road.

Jess caught her first glimpse of the lake through the trees.

She slowed down when she saw the road flares lined along the shoulder.

A flagman was just up ahead and waved for her to stop.

"I'm afraid you're going to have to turn around," the flagman said, approaching her side window.

"You don't understand. I have to get through," Jess said.

"Not possible. Last night's storm brought the hill down on the road. No one gets in or out. Might be another two or three days before we can get it cleared."

"Is there another way in?" Jess asked.

"Nope. Not unless you can chopper in."

"How far is the lake from here?" Jess asked, wondering if she should hike in.

"A good six or seven miles, I'd say."

"I see." That ruled that out.

"You can turn around over there," the flagman said, pointing to a wide area on the shoulder of the road.

Jess followed the flagman's instructions. She could see the bulldozers at work, scooping up the mud; the hillside looking like it could come down at any minute.

The asphalt ended at the wall of mud like it was meant to dead-end there.

She turned around and headed back, not sure what she should do next.

After driving a mile, she pulled the Bronco over to the side of the road. She got out and walked over to the edge and studied the terrain below. As treacherous as it was, Jess knew she had no other choice if she wanted to get to the lake. She would have to pick the best route and take her chances.

After a two-minute search, she found the right spot. The grade was not as steep, but there were plenty of trees to dodge. It was impossible to tell from this distance if the Bronco would even fit between some of those trees. There was only one way to find out.

Jess got back in the Bronco, started the engine, and positioned the vehicle perpendicular to the road, blocking one lane. It was a dangerous thing to do considering she was close to a blind curve.

She put the transmission lever on the steering column into neutral, reached down, and pulled the four-wheel drive shift on the floorboard into 4L. The four-wheel drive display lit up on the dashboard, signifying that the four-wheel transmission was engaged.

She dropped the lever on the steering column into low. The Bronco idled. She was nervous as hell, mustering the courage—

A pickup truck barreled around the bend.

The surprised driver blasted his horn. He locked up his brakes, and the rear tires screeched and smoked.

The truck came at her like a torpedo, ready to broadside the Bronco.

Leaving Jess no time but to react.

Jess tromped on the accelerator. For an instance, all she could see was gray sky and treetops through the windshield—and then the Bronco shot out over the edge and plunged down.

She stood on the brake pedal with both feet. The Bronco careened down the slick slope. She frantically wrestled the wheel, dodging trees rushing up.

Branches slapped the windshield and clawed the fenders.

The all-terrain tires slipped in the mud, forcing the Bronco to go sideways, robbing Jess's control of the vehicle, then miraculously regained traction.

The Bronco bottomed out, and a wave of mud splashed over the hood, splattering the windshield.

CHAPTER EIGHT

"Come on, Devon," Nell shouted, waiting impatiently at the head of the stairs.

"Hold your horses," Devon replied. He gathered some towels under his arm and strode across the deck. He wore sunglasses, a straw Stetson, and a zipped-up gray sweatshirt over his ski wetsuit, the neoprene covering his thighs, leaving the rest of his legs exposed.

The morning sky was a smoky gray with billowing dismal clouds, but at least it was not raining for the time being.

Devon followed his sister down the stairs leading to the cove.

"One, two, three," Nell said, counting off the steps.

She stopped on the last step but could not go any further without stepping into the lake. She looked up at Devon with a perplexed expression. "Eighteen? Hey! How come there are only eighteen steps instead of twenty-two?"

"Must have rained pretty hard last night," he said. "The other steps are under the water."

Devon hoisted Nell on his shoulder and waded out to the boat.

Sean was already onboard. He was wearing a light-blue ski wetsuit. A huge inner tube was wedged in the back seat next to the black engine cover.

"Do we need to bail?" Devon asked Sean. He lifted Nell over the gunwale. Nell was wearing a life preserver over a heavy jacket and sweat clothes.

"Nope, the tarp kept the Pumpkin Eater as dry as a bone."

The McNeeley's had had the Pumpkin Eater for years. The Sidewinder was painted a bright orange with black, tuck-and-roll upholstered seats. A 289 cubic-inch V-8 engine was concealed under the engine cover, and the craft was propelled by an inboard/outboard. Despite its age, the boat looked sleek and racy. Many times other boaters would come alongside and challenge him to a race. Devon usually obliged.

Devon untied the rope anchored to a stake and tossed it ashore.

"Max, here boy!" Devon called, wading in the water with one hand on the boat.

Max ran down the bank and dove in the lake. The golden retriever was wearing a flotation vest with a handle. As soon as Max was within reach, Devon grabbed the handle and lifted the sixty-pound dog into the boat and then climbed in after.

Devon sat behind the steering wheel. He held a key with a small yellow rubber float attached—in the event the key was to fall in the water—with the catch phrase: 'Right or Wrong, I'm Still The Captain!'

He put the key in the ignition, started the engine, and the boat fired up, rumbling like a beefy roadster.

"Hold on!" Devon gunned the boat out of the cove. The bow popped up out of the water. As the Pumpkin Eater gained speed, the bow dropped down and began cutting a wedge through the water as the boat trimmed out.

Devon let her rip. He gave the boat full throttle and steered for the middle of the lake. Nell sat beside him, the wind blowing her hair. Sean sat in one of the back seats, holding onto the inner tube so that the wind wouldn't blow it out of the boat.

Devon studied the lake ahead. The rain had swollen the lake. Some of the islands that had existed before had disappeared. Whenever he saw a bush sticking out of the water, he knew that there was land only a few feet below the surface. He made sure to steer clear of them.

"Are we out far enough?" Sean asked.

Devon could tell his brother was anxious to get in the water.

"This should do," Devon said, slowing down the boat. He switched off the ignition key, stopping the propeller.

The Pumpkin Eater rocked in a soothing rhythm, the rough water around it beginning to quell.

Sean snapped on his ski vest and jumped in the lake.

Nell stood up in the boat and was holding a bright orange flag to signal other boaters that they had someone in the water, even though there were no other boats to be seen.

Max jumped up and rested his front paws on the gunwale, whining because Sean was in the water.

"He's okay. Relax, Max," Devon said. Max stopped his crying but never took his eyes off of Sean.

"Man, it's cold," Sean said, swimming in a tight circle to generate heat inside his wetsuit.

Devon threw the inner tube out into the water. A ski rope was attached to the inner tube and tied off to a plated ring mounted on a stanchion above the engine cover.

"I'm going to take out the slack," Devon warned. He made sure Sean was clear of the prop before starting the engine.

Devon throttled forward slowly, until the towline was drawn taut.

"So Nell, what's your job?" Devon asked, always big on safety.

"I'm the spotter. If Sean falls, I tell you he's down and we go back around."

"That's right. Let me know when he's ready?"

Devon glanced over his shoulder.

Sean pulled himself on the inner tube and grabbed the handle of the ski rope.

He raised his arm.

"Hit it!" Nell yelled.

Devon gave the boat full throttle. The boat took off slow at first then leveled out when it was going fast enough to compensate for the weight of the drag from the inner tube it was towing.

Sean clung to the bouncing inner tube caught in the boat's choppy wake.

He shifted his weight and gained control. He rode the inner tube out of the wake and onto the flat lake.

Usually, this time of day, the lake would be as smooth as glass, but this morning, the surface was rippling, though calm enough for some excellent tubing.

Devon headed out for Grizzly Island, keeping the speedometer at thirty miles per hour. He leaned back, glancing back occasionally as Sean traversed back and forth across the wake of the boat. Sean held up his arm and made a circular motion.

"Sean wants us to whip him," Nell said.

Max watched Sean from one of the back seats. The dog's ears and the hair on the dome of his head ruffled in the wind.

Devon sat up straight so he could get a clear line of sight of the lake ahead and saw nothing ahead but flat water.

"Here we go, brace yourself. Grab hold of Max."

Nell called Max and he came over. She grabbed the handle on his vest.

Devon cut the wheel to the left and powered the boat.

He glanced back at the towline and saw Sean gradually whip out from behind the boat until he was almost perpendicular to the starboard side. The inner tube gained incredible speed, skimming over the water, actually going faster than the Pumpkin Eater.

"Woooyaaaa!" Sean hollered as the inner tube shot over the water.

After completing a full loop, Devon straightened out the boat and throttled down. Sean scooted off the inner tube and slipped into the lake.

Devon circled around to pick up Sean. Nell held the flag above her head.

"That was intense," Sean yelled, floating on his back as the boat approached.

The inner tube trailed behind the boat like a forgotten dingy.

Devon turned off the ignition. He made sure to keep the ski rope clear of the stern of the boat so he wouldn't suck it up in the prop. Sean swam to the inboard/outboard drive and used it for a step to climb into the back of the boat.

"My turn," Devon said. He took off his sweatshirt, put on his ski vest, and slipped on a pair of ski gloves, roughed up on the palms to give him a firm grip on the inner tube.

"You're the skipper." Devon handed his sunglasses and cowboy hat to Sean.

Without hesitation, Devon jumped into the water. Sean had been right. The water was freezing. He vigorously kicked his legs, swimming backward to warm up his muscles.

Devon did the sidestroke out to the inner tube. With one hand on the inner tube, he raised his other hand to signal for Sean to take out the slack. He watched Nell turn to communicate his request to Sean. The engine started, and the boat slowly idled forward.

Soon, the towline was taut and the boat began to drag the inner tube over the water. Once the inner tube was stable enough, Devon lurched aboard and grabbed hold of the ski handle that knotted the rope to the inner tube. It was difficult to balance at this slow speed. The inner tube wobbled in the slight wake threatening to flip him over if he was not careful.

"Hit it!" Devon yelled. The boat roared ahead, churning the water behind the Sidewinder's stern.

Devon clutched the handle of the ski rope in his right hand and used his left to widen the base of his center of gravity. Using his hips to shift his weight, Devon could also drag his feet in the water, acting as a rudder.

The inner tube contorted into an oval shape and plowed through the water. Once there was enough speed, the inner tube returned to its original shape and began to glide over the boat's wake. Water flew up through the doughnut hole and slapped Devon in the stomach. He had to squint, the onrushing wake splashing in his face.

Even though Devon was an expert water skier on a single ski, he always enjoyed the rush he got from tubing. It was akin to body surfing in the ocean, shooting the curl headfirst, like getting a surfboard's-eye view coming off of a wave.

After a couple of minutes of slaloming the boat's wake, Devon raised his hand with his thumb extended upward signaling that he wanted Sean to speed up.

The Pumpkin Eater began to go faster.

The ride got bumpier. Devon began to make the inner tube jump the sloping waves left by the boat. He made a couple daredevil maneuvers, almost losing it once when he went airborne.

It was time for the whip. He waved his arm in the air.

The ski boat banked to the left. For a moment, the inner tube seemed trapped in the concave center of the wake. Devon leaned to the right. The inner tube rose and flew down the outside wash onto the flat water. Devon held on tighter, shifting his weight to the left, the centrifugal force trying to peel him off.

His face was only six inches above the water, racing over the surface at forty miles an hour. At this speed, if he hit the water wrong, the impact would be akin to taking a belly flop onto a cement driveway.

The inner tube went faster, hydroplaning over the water.

Devon spotted something in the water ahead. It was hard to see clearly with the spray in his face, but it looked like a log—directly in his path. He tried to react in time, but he was too late.

The inner tube smacked into the log, and Devon was flipped off.

The next few seconds were a blur, but the pain was not. He toppled over on the rock-hard water. Dazed, he floated on his back, the impact having bruised his ribs despite the padded ski vest.

"Devon, are you okay?" Nell shouted from the boat as they came around. Sean gave the engine a short burst of power then switched off the ignition, allowing the vessel to drift up to Devon.

"What happened?" Sean asked, leaning over the side.

"Are you blind? Didn't you see that log?" Devon grumbled, swimming for the stern.

"What log?"

Devon pulled himself into the boat.

"There!" Devon said, pointing to the log drifting in the water.

Max began to growl. The hackles on his scruff stood straight up. It was a menacing growl, tinged with fear. Max was generally good-tempered. This was not normal behavior for the golden retriever. Max barked, whined, then barked again growling in between.

"Devon, I'm scared," Nell said, trying her best to hold on to Max.

"Pull in the inner tube," Devon snapped.

Sean ambled to the stern of the boat.

Max continued to growl, pacing from one side of the boat to the other, jumping onto the gunwale with his front paws.

"What's wrong with you?" Devon had to restrain Max by the handle to prevent the dog from lunging over the side. Sean hoisted the inner tube into the boat.

"I'll drive," Devon said, snatching his sunglasses and Stetson from Sean.

Devon revved the Pumpkin Eater and jammed back to the resort.

***

Kate had just set lunch on the table when Sean and Nell strolled in.

"So, did you both have fun?"

"Yeah, a regular blast," Sean said sarcastically and went to his room.

"What's with him?" Kate asked Nell.

"He and Devon got into it, as usual," Nell said.

"Well, after he cools off, tell him he better eat. When you've both finished, come down to the store. Sean has work to do, and you have studying to catch up on."

"Oh, Mom!"

"Knowledge is food for the brain, just like that sandwich is food for your tummy."

"That's corny," Nell said, sitting up to the table.

"Maybe so, but it's true. See you in a bit," Kate said. She grabbed her jacket and went out the door.

Ten minutes later, Kate was inside the store, switching on the lights. She went over and turned on the portable TV on the end of the counter.

She was about to check the shelves when the television drew her attention.

The screen showed a woman news reporter dressed in rainwear holding a microphone up to her chin. She was conducting an interview.

"This is Victoria Savage in Madison. We are here at the Murdock Fish Hatchery. With me is Billy Garner, foreman of the hatchery. Mr. Garner, would you describe to us what happened here last night?" The camera panned right of the news reporter to the man standing next to her.

"It was damn scary, is what it was. We were down in that ravine, laying out sandbags when the levee broke. We were lucky to get out of there alive."

"Was there much damage?"

"Well, we lost three of the ponds."

"You mean the ones to our right?" Victoria Savage asked. The camera panned over to the ponds and back to the reporter.

"Yes, we lost over two thousand pounds of catfish."

"My goodness. But, I only see two ponds, Mr. Garner. Is that the other pond over there?" Again, the camera moved away, this time focusing on the collapsed wall behind a Quonset hut.

"Ah, yeah." The camera had returned to Mr. Garner.

"And what was kept there?"

The hatchery foreman hesitated, unsure what he should say next.

"Mr. Garner?"

"Catfish, I believe."

Kate's television screen switched to the network's studio, where a newscaster with too much stage makeup sat behind a well-polished countertop.

"Victoria? What can you tell us about the break in the levee?"

A picture-in-picture display showed on the background behind and above the newscaster's left shoulder so that the viewers could watch him and Victoria Savage simultaneously.

The reporter walked to her right and stopped. Just behind her, but still in plain view, was the levee with a torrential rush of water flowing through a gap in the embankment.

There were bulldozers and a caravan of dump trucks on the scene.

"As you can see, John, the Corp of Engineers has their work cut out for them. Everything hinges on the Sacramento River…and what she will do next. It could be another day or two before the waterline of the river drops enough so that the levee can be shored up. Only problem is…they are predicting another storm front to hit here later this afternoon. All we can do now is *wait*…and *pray*…that the rain lets up. This is Victoria Savage. Back to you, John."

The picture-in-picture of Victoria Savage dissolved.

"Thank you, Victoria," John said. "We have a news breaking story of another incident of road rage reported on the interstate. Sam Wright, a landscaper from Madison, suffered a gunshot wound to the shoulder when another motorist opened fire on Mr. Wright's car. Apparently, Mr. Wright was returning home from work when he was shot.

"The California Highway Patrol is alerting motorists to be on the lookout for a dark-colored four-door sedan. This could be another assault by the *Highway Marauder,* who is responsible for five other attacks on motorists in the past few weeks. Now, for the weather…"

"Hello, Kate."

Kate turned her attention away from the television and was taken aback by the woman standing by the front door. She had been so engrossed with the news report that she had not heard the bell ring.

"I'm afraid business is going to be slow for a while," Jess Murdock said.

"And why's that?"

"The road is closed. Mudslide."

"Then, how did you get here?" Kate asked.

"Let's say, I had to improvise." Jess glanced out the store's front window.

Kate looked out and saw a vehicle parked outside completely covered in mud.

"Well, that frees up my day. Would you care for some coffee?"

"Yes, I could use some caffeine right about now," Jess said. "You haven't by any chance seen my brother, Vernon?"

"Is that why you are here?"

"It's important that I find him."

"I haven't seen him," Kate said and poured two cups of coffee. She handed a cup to Jess. "Let's go sit outside and talk."

The women went outside and sat at a table overlooking the lake.

"I love it out here," Kate said, sipping her coffee.

Kate and Jess bided their time, not saying a word.

Finally, Kate opened with, "I wish I had..." Just as Jess blurted, "I didn't know how..."

They both stopped and smiled at each other.

"A lot has changed," Jess said.

"I know."

"I don't know if you heard, but I took over my grandfather's business when he died."

"The hatchery?"

"Yes. It was a go at first, but I do enjoy it."

"Must keep you busy."

"Oh, you can't believe."

"So busy that you didn't have time for my son?"

"Kate, you don't understand."

"Explain it to me."

"It's true, I've missed Devon. But I've been struggling to keep the hatchery in operation, not to mention worrying about my brother. Which is really why I'm here. To find Vernon."

"And why do you think he's here?"

"I've been following his trail." Jess reached inside her purse and pulled out the journal, which she held up and said, "This belongs to Vernon. I'm pretty sure it has to do with his research."

"Research?"

"Something he's been working on. I'm not completely sure."

"Perhaps you should talk to Jonathan."

"Jonathan?"

"Jonathan Stone."

"You mean Professor Jonathan Stone? The ichthyologist? He used to be one of our professors."

"Well, it really is a small world."

CHAPTER NINE

Victoria Savage handed her microphone to Bernie Barnes, her audio technician, stepping into the news van. He crawled to the rear of the van to stow the rest of his sound gear.

Tony Carver, Savage's cameraman, was sitting on a swivel chair in front of a console of monitors and communication equipment inside the van. He switched off the feed that had just broadcasted Victoria's live interview.

"How did I look?" she asked Tony. She had spent two minutes preparing her script for the interview and twenty minutes fixing her makeup and hair.

"Beautiful as always," he replied.

Victoria loved the spotlight. Aspiring to work her way up to an anchor position, she had eagerly taken any assignment dished out to her to get exposure on the broadcast news. All she needed was to cover a big story, one that would get her recognition from the network executives. It was inevitable that Barbara Walters and Diane Sawyer would be stepping down someday, and when that day came, Victoria would be standing in the wings to fill in.

So far, nothing had come her way.

Nearly all of her airtime had been reporting El Nino related stories while she stood in the freezing rain, usually at 4:00 a.m., yelling into the microphone while a calamity ensued behind her.

She wondered if the viewers really appreciated the sacrifices she made just so that they could conveniently get their daily dosage of the news and be able to go to work and have something to talk about during their coffee breaks. She knew the viewers couldn't give a rat's ass about her. She was just another pretty face for the camera.

"Did you notice how the foreman reacted when I asked him about that pond by the Quonset hut?" Victoria asked Tony.

"He was just shook up from last night," Tony replied, adjusting the tracking on one of the video recorders.

"Maybe, but I don't think so. Call it a hunch," Victoria said.

Tony shook his head and went back to fiddling with his controls.

"I'm serious. There is something strange about that place," she said, eyeing the Quonset hut.

"What's so strange about a dilapidated shack?"

"Tony, I want you to go over and check it out."

"Shouldn't I get the foreman's permission first?"

"What for?"

"It's policy to—"

"Forget all that. Just do it. Get moving."

"You know, we could get canned for trespassing."

"Not if we don't get caught. Hell, if every news reporter played it safe, there wouldn't be any news. Go," Victoria said, shooing Tony out of the van.

Tony reluctantly climbed out. He pulled up the hood on his windbreaker, shoved his hands into his pockets, and casually strolled toward the Quonset hut.

"Where's Tony going?" asked Bernie, stepping out of the van.

"Wait, you'll see," Victoria said. One aspect of her job that she liked was the power she had over her crew. Tony and Bernie were always willing to oblige—not that Victoria was putting out—as she had them wrapped around her little finger.

They knew that their jobs were as stable as a three-legged coffee table when it came to the media job market. If sticking with Victoria was going to keep them employed, all the merrier.

"Hey, look," Bernie said, pointing to Tony sneaking into Quonset hut.

"Don't point, you idiot," Victoria said and slapped his arm.

"Ouch."

"Just act natural."

Victoria and Bernie pretended to stow their equipment so as not to look suspicious.

"I thought you all had left?" a gruff voice said.

Victoria turned and saw a large man standing in front of her. A masticated cigar hung out of the corner of his mouth.

"Oh, we're almost packed up," Victoria said.

"That's some fancy gear you got there," the man said.

Victoria stole a peek at the Quonset hut. Tony was just coming out the door.

"Would you like to take a closer look…mister?"

"The name's Gus. Sure."

Victoria quickly took Gus by the arm and dragged him over to the van so he would not see Tony.

"So, what does all of this do?" Gus asked.

"This is where we do our editing, satellite uplinks, communicate with the networks, that sort of thing," she said, stalling.

"Technical stuff, eh?"

"You bet."

"Hey, wasn't there another feller with you?" asked Gus. He stepped away from the van and started to look around.

"I'm back," Tony said, walking out from behind the van. He looked at Gus and said, "Had to use the can. We better shove off."

"It was nice to have met you, Gus," Victoria said, climbing into the back of the van. Tony jumped in behind her. He smiled at Gus then shut the sliding door.

Bernie got behind the wheel, started the van, and drove off.

Victoria waved to Gus through the rear windows.

CHAPTER TEN

Sean dropped Nell off at the store then drove the golf cart down to the marina. He stormed out on the berth, still angry at Devon.

Can't I ever do anything right in his eyes?

He hated being the younger brother, always having to take the abuse. He had been responsible and careful driving the boat.

And what was up with that log? It just seemed to appear out of nowhere. Or, maybe Devon was making it up. Sure, there may have been a log, but had Devon really hit it?

Maybe Devon just freaked out and blew the ride.

Yeah, and that is why he was so pissed. Devon just wanted someone to blame because he screwed up. Talk about lame.

Sean was beginning to feel better already.

***

Max loped around behind the Fallow trailer, sniffed the garbage can, then ran around the front. Barking twice, he scampered off and hid, waiting for Rosie. He took a moment and gave himself a vigorous scratch.

He was about to wander off to chase a butterfly when Rosie burst out of the doggie door.

Excited with the arrival of his playmate, Max spun around twice then took off in a strong run. Rosie raced after him. Twenty pounds lighter than Max, Rosie could still keep up with Max.

They ran for a few minutes, arriving at the beach at Landon Cove.

Never timid, Max dove into the water. He paddled out a short distance then returned. Rose wagged her tail and jumped in the water. She swam in a circle and came back ashore.

The golden retriever ran gracefully with his chest thrust out, his feathered tail erect, his powerful legs carrying him majestically up to the campground.

Max spotted the ashen remains in a campfire pit and rolled in it. He especially enjoyed wallowing on his back, kicking his legs in the air.

Rose ran up and mimicked Max. Soon, they were both covered in ash from head to tail. Filthy, the dogs darted off.

They paused for a breather at the chain-link fence that kept campers from wandering into the dam site. Max hunkered down into a burrow he had made beforehand and crawled beneath the fence, leading the way for Rosie.

The dogs trotted toward the first cave. Max went in about ten feet and began to bark. Each bark echoed back from the dark depths of the cavern. Rosie also barked, her ears perked upright at the sound of the dog answering her back.

Max and Rosie sprinted for the next cave and went inside. They started barking. The dogs that lived in the cave, but were never seen, replied.

A loud guttural gasp bellowed from the cave.

Both dogs retreated, yelping as they ran.

Max led the way up the hillside toward the dam. Once they were on the summit, Max turned and growled. Rosie nestled up against him.

Max backed up, watching the cave below.

He sauntered over to the entrance of the diversion tunnel.

The mouth of the tunnel was almost twenty feet in diameter; sealed off by an eight-foot wall of sheets of industrial plywood, meant to keep curious intruders out.

Faded signs: *Keep Out, No Trespassing,* and *Danger Area* were posted on the weathered plywood. Tumbleweeds had gathered at the base of the entrance.

A flurry of quail flew out from the dried brush.

Max was startled and reared back, losing his footing on the concrete slope of the dam's base.

His toenails clicked on the steep cement.

Unable to get a hold, Max slid down the six-foot concrete precipice, rolled backward, and splashed into the lake.

Stunned, he paddled through a maze of floating debris drifting on the greenish froth caused by the storm. He frantically pawed at the water unable to see above a jam of logs blocking his vision of the shore.

The more Max tried to find his way, the further out he went.

Rosie looked down from the crest of the dam and whined while Max paddled off in the wrong direction.

CHAPTER ELEVEN

"So, what did you find?" Victoria asked Tony. They were both sitting on the swivel chairs at the communication console.

"A mess. Looked like there was a fire. Charred computer equipment, water damage everywhere. It was a regular pigsty. I think it used to be a laboratory. I did find these," Tony said. He reached under his windbreaker and took out a folded map, a letter, and videotape.

"I found the letter on a bed in the back. Looked like someone was living in there."

"Let me see that," Victoria said. Tony handed her the letter. "It's an official correspondence from an investor to a Vernon Murdock," she said, perusing the letter. She skipped down, then read, "...and it is with deep regret that we must inform you that due to your inability to comply with the agreement stated within our contract, all funds are to be terminated forthwith."

"What agreement?" Tony asked.

"It doesn't say. Where did you find the tape?"

"It was still in the VCR. The recorder looked thrashed, but the tape might still work. Let's take a look." Tony slipped the tape inside one of the video players on the console and punched rewind.

"So, what's the map of?" Victoria asked.

"It's a topography map, I know that."

Victoria opened up the map and spread it out on the narrow workspace reserved for note taking and the keyboards.

"Looks like Murdock marked it up," she said, tracing her finger along the black ink drawn on the map. "It's a route from the hatchery to some lake. Lake Recluse. Ever hear of it?"

"No."

The VCR made a clunking sound. The tape had rewound.

"Let's see what we have here," Tony said, hitting the play button.

The monitor screen went static with a snowy pattern. They watched for a few minutes with anticipation, but the picture remained the same.

"Probably ruined from the fire," Tony said, but left the tape running.

Victoria looked out the windshield and saw that they were on the freeway.

Suddenly, there was a loud explosion and the van rocked. Bernie fought to keep the van on the road and then pulled off to the shoulder.

"Flat tire," he said, and climbed out to take a look.

"Oh, this is great. Just great!" Victoria said.

The sliding door opened.

"Let me through so I can get the jack," Bernie said. Victoria and Tony cleared a path. Bernie rummaged in the back and came crawling back with a tire iron and the jack.

"You two mind getting out," he said, stepping out of the van.

Victoria and Tony got out and stood by the opened door.

"Hey, look," Tony said.

Victoria glanced over at the monitor. The static picture had disappeared, revealing a man standing on the catwalk inside the Quonset hut. Below him was the concrete extension that connected to the exterior pond.

"That must be Murdock," Tony said, stepping up to get a closer look at the screen.

"What's he looking at?" Victoria could see the cloudy water in the extension.

Then her eyes started playing tricks on her. There was something in the water—and it was huge.

"What the hell is that?" she said.

"I'd say that was one big-ass fish."

The screen went fuzzy again.

"Play that back," Victoria said. Tony reached in and pressed rewind.

"We need to get to that lake," Victoria said. "Bernie, what's the holdup?"

Bernie came around from the back of the van.

"I've got some bad news," he said.

"What? There's no spare?" Victoria asked.

"Oh, there's a spare all right, but it's flatter than the tire that just blew. We passed a service station about a mile back," Bernie said. "I'll walk the spare back and get it fixed. I'm sure I can get a lift back. Shouldn't take more than an hour."

"You do that," Victoria said then turned to Tony. "Let's look at that tape again."

***

Professor Stone swept the leaves on his patio. He looked in the washtub expecting carp, but the basin was empty.

"Rosie! Here snookums. Come to Momma," called Liz, strolling down the road.

"Ran off again, has she?" Professor Stone said, leaning on the porch railing.

"I don't know what gets into her," Liz said.

"Don't fret. She'll be back before you know it."

"I hope so."

"Looks like we're going to get some more rain," Professor Stone said, glancing up at the inclement sky. A slight wind picked up, disturbing the small pile of leaves.

"I hate for her to be out in this weather."

"She'll be fine. You better get back inside."

"I suppose you're right. Thank you, Jonathan." Liz walked back in the direction of her trailer.

"Bye, Liz."

Professor Stone took his broom and scooted the remaining pile of leaves off the deck.

He was about to go back inside when a truck pulled up. He wondered when was the last time the owner had bothered to wash it. The driver climbed out.

"Professor," Jess Murdock said.

"Oh my lord. Jess. It's been a long time. How are you?"

Jess said she was fine and explained the reason for her visit.

"Please, come inside."

Jess sat down at the kitchen table and placed the bag down in front of her.

"I haven't seen your brother."

"Then perhaps you can help me with this." Jess pulled a thick book from the bag.

She handed the book to Professor Stone.

At first, the professor thought it was an accountant's ledger.

"Before you try to make heads or tails out of it, I need to tell you some things," Jess said.

Professor Stone listened as Jess started her story. While she talked, his eyes kept drifting to the front cover of the book in his hands, and the words: *The Silurid Result.*

CHAPTER TWELVE

The rain had diminished to a light drizzle for the time being.

Vernon sat cross-legged under a rigged lean-to fashioned from a tarp tied to a tree to stay dry, warming himself by a small campfire.

Behind him was his truck.

The front grill was buried into the ground, the hood buckled. The windshield had been completely smashed out. He vaguely remembered skidding off the road to avoid hitting a deer and careening down through the trees in the dark.

He'd escaped injury during last night's crash except for a gash on the top of his head. After a while, he'd used the portable pump and inflated the raft. But once he hooked up the gas line to the outboard motor, the fumes had given him a headache, so he had decided to sleep.

The nightmares haunted him, eventually waking him up.

Vernon adjusted the dial on the portable tracking device. He wished he had thought to recharge the battery. He had spent an hour reconfiguring the display so that it would represent the circumference of the lake, rather than the perimeter of the pond back at the hatchery. He cursed himself for not bringing the map, having to make his adjustments from memory.

He turned on the unit.

Two blips came on the screen.

Zeus and Athena were still alive.

***

"And what does the word *ecology* mean?" Kate asked, helping Nell with her studies at her table behind the store's counter.

"It's how we learn to live together and not spoil the land," Nell replied, fidgeting in her chair.

"Good answer. What is a *dominant species*?"

Nell thought for a moment.

"An animal that is stronger and meaner that the other animals. And eats all their food."

"Good! Well, that should do for today." Kate figured with the road closed, there was no point in keeping the store open. Besides, it was almost time to prepare dinner.

"I thought we'd never be done," Nell said, jumping out of her chair.

"Go down and tell your brother dinner will be ready in an hour."

"Sure, Mom." Nell ran out of the store like a critter that had just gnawed itself free from a trap.

***

"That's incredible," Professor Stone said, once Jess was through. He held the book differently now, almost reverently. He knew the pages within held a remarkable discovery.

"I need time to study this. Can you give me a couple of hours?"

"Sure. I'm going to look for Vernon."

"You might ask Devon to help you. Maybe he's seen your brother."

Jess paused at the door then left without saying a word.

***

Bernie arrived back at the van three hours later, pushing the same flat tire.

"Where the hell have you been?" Victoria shouted.

"Hey, I thought it was only a mile. I was wrong. When I finally got to the station, the damn place was closed. So, I tried hitching a ride back, but do you think anyone would pick me up. Hell no! That Highway Marauder has everyone spooked. Nobody trusts anyone these days. So, don't be yelling at me," Bernie said, and kicked the tire.

"We've wasted valuable time. If I knew you were going to be so long..." Victoria paused. It was late in the afternoon and she was tired from being up since three in the morning. A hot shower and some clean clothes were in order, but they would have to wait.

She reached into her purse and pulled out her cellular phone.

"What, you let me walk all that way and you had that damn thing the whole time!"

"Don't turn this around on me. It was your idea to take off with that tire. Besides, do you have any idea of what minutes cost these days?"

"Man, I don't believe it," Bernie said.

"That'll teach you for gallivanting all over the countryside."

"Tony, I'm going to kill her."

"Save it for later. Right now, we need some help," Tony said. "It's going to be dark soon. I don't want to get lost out here."

***

Jess walked out on the dock, daylight waning into dusk. She approached the boathouse, found the door ajar, and peered inside the dimly lit structure.

The only light was a cone-shaded bulb dangling from a rafter, shining down on a workbench cluttered with engine parts, gears, and propellers. Screwdrivers, wrenches, pliers, and various other tools hung on a pegboard.

Two fifty-gallon drums, filled with water, stood in one corner. An outboard motor was mounted on the rim of one of the drums. The engine belched blue smoke while the propeller churned up the water inside the drum.

Double doors closed off a vacant slip used for repairing a boat while it was still in the water.

Devon was working on the carburetor of an outboard engine at the workbench. He began fastening the engine cover back in place. He picked up a Philips head screwdriver, placed a screw on the end, and tried to line up the threads. The screw slipped out and fell on the floorboards.

"Oh, hell," he said, bending down to search for the screw.

"Here, I have it," Jess said, snatching the screw before it fell through a gap between the floorboards.

Devon looked at her as if she were a ghost. The shocked look on his face quickly transformed into a perplexed stare. He stood up and leaned against the workbench.

"Aren't you going to say something?" Jess asked, standing up.

"What am I supposed to say? Hell, Jess."

"I know it's been awhile."

"That's an understatement," Devon said sarcastically.

"Somehow, I thought you might act this way."

"What did you expect? You stop coming around, and suddenly, you just drop in like it's nothing." Devon grabbed a rag and began rubbing the grease from his hands.

"Devon. I've just been so—"

"Busy? Yeah, I get it. I guess I was a fool to think that we would ever get married, raise a family together."

"Oh, Devon. That's exactly why I couldn't come back." Jess fought back the tears.

"What?"

"A family."

"What are you talking about?"

"When would I have time with the hatchery, worrying about Vernon…?"

Devon stood silent, his hands worrying the shop rag.

"I better leave," Jess said, turning away.

"We could still be a family: you and me."

Jess paused at the door.

"Who says you have to have kids. Heck, I have a dog. Well, he's the family dog but…" Devon smiled. He took her arm and pulled her toward him. He put his hand up to her face and kissed her.

Jess put her arms around his waist, squeezed him so hard that he let out a little gasp when their lips parted.

"Sorry, grease," Devon said. He grabbed a clean rag from the workbench and wiped her cheek. She reached up, closed her eyes, and kissed him again.

The boathouse trembled.

"Did you feel that?" Jess asked, opening her eyes. She glanced down at their shadows cast along the floor and saw them moving due to the overhead light swinging back and forth.

"You bet," Devon said, his eyes still closed.

Another jolt shook the boathouse. The tools on the pegboard rattled and water sloshed out of the fifty-gallon drums.

"What was that? Felt like an earthquake," Devon said, opening his eyes.

"That wasn't an earthquake," Jess said.

The floorboards beneath their feet suddenly buckled upward. Thrown to the floor, Jess and Devon got drenched when the heavy drums toppled over.

The outboard motor struck the floor. The engine spun around out of control, the blades of the propeller chopping along the wood planks. Jess was about to push herself up from the floor when she saw the propeller coming straight for her face.

She rolled out of the propeller's path.

Devon caught up with the runaway outboard motor and hit the kill switch.

Jess saw something emerge in the slip.

Algae-green and sleek, it was enormous. Patterned plates covered the massive body. She tried to gauge its length as it undulated through the water. It was at least thirty feet in length.

The creature buckled the decking and ripped the boards from the rear wall of the boathouse with its thrashing fluked tail.

Devon ran over and grabbed Jess.

The monster scraped the bottom of the doors of the slip and tore them from their hinges.

And then it submerged and was gone.

"What was that?" Devon asked.

"I don't know, but I think we are about to find out," Jess said.

CHAPTER THIRTEEN

"Where could he be? It's getting dark," Nell said.

"This isn't like Max to be gone this long," Sean said, wishing that they had started their search sooner, having not seen Max for most of the afternoon.

Sean thought that Max might be over at Landon Cove, but he'd been wrong. They had scouted the south shore with no luck. That is when Sean decided to cut across the lake to see if Max was over by the creeks.

They were in the middle of the lake when the noisy 5-horsepower outboard motor shook the transom, sputtered, and died. Sean tried restarting the engine, but it refused to fire up.

"What's wrong with it?" Nell asked.

"I don't believe it," Sean said, hitting the motor with his fist.

"Don't tell me we're out of gas."

"Okay, I won't tell you."

"Then you better start rowing," Nell said.

"Who made you skipper?" Sean snapped. He took the oars and slipped them into the oarlocks. He tilted the motor up to raise the propeller out of the water.

Sean paddled one oar in the water to turn the boat around.

The lights in the trailer park were about a mile away.

"Man, it's going to take us forever to get back. What else could go wrong?" Sean said as he rowed.

The sprinkling rain stiffened into a steady downpour.

"That'll teach me to keep my mouth shut," Sean said.

That's when they heard a dog howling in the night.

"It's Max," Nell said.

"How did he get way out here?"

"I don't know. You don't think Mom is going to be mad we took the boat?"

"Not if we find Max. You know how she loves that dog." Sean put his shoulders into the oars.

***

Liz Fallow zipped up her pink raincoat. She was worried about Rosie. It was not like Rosie to be gone for so long and not be home in time for supper. Liz checked her flashlight. It seemed to be working fine.

She closed the front door behind her and went outside.

"Miserable rain," she mumbled, climbing into her pink golf cart. Pink tassels ran along the inside lip of the cab's roof.

She decided to drive around the trailer park then check along the shoreline until she found Rosie. She turned the key on the golf cart and proceeded down the road.

No treats for you tonight, you naughty girl, for making Mommy worry!

***

Kate removed the roast from the table and put it in the microwave oven to keep warm. *Why aren't those kids home, yet?* She thought to herself. They were always prompt for dinner, even if the menu was not to their liking. Her rump roast was their favorite.

She heard a knock, walked over, and opened the front door.

"Hi, Kate. Did you know the road is closed?" Kelly said, shaking the rain off before she stepped inside. "I tried going to class, but the road is blocked off due to a mudslide."

"I know," Kate said, closing the door after Kelly.

"Was it on the news?"

"No. Jess told me," Kate said.

"Who's Jess?" asked Kelly.

"Someone that Devon used to date after high school years ago. You haven't seen Sean or Nell, have you?"

"No."

"Could you do me a favor?"

"Sure."

"I need to go over to Jonathan's. Call me when those kids get in."

"Will do."

"See you in a bit," Kate said, grabbing her coat.

Outside, Kate flipped her hood over her head. She stepped down from the deck and turned on her flashlight. She walked over to the stairs that led down to the beach hoping that she would see Sean and Nell. She directed the beam of the torch down, tracking the light along the beach. Only there wasn't a sandy beach anymore, only water.

The lake was rising.

She shined the light on the steps. She counted only ten steps to the water. But how could that be?

Kate flashed back to the newscast about the levee breaking. Of course, the runoff from the levee was filling the lake.

Stark realization hit her like a mallet. Unless the levee was repaired—and damn fast—the trailer park would soon be flooded.

***

Jess and Devon walked up to Professor Stone's trailer and knocked on the door. They heard a voice call out, "Come in," and they went inside.

Professor Stone was standing in the middle of his living room, surrounded by fish tanks. He held Vernon's journal tightly to his chest like a priest clutching a prayer book. He seemed to be in a trance-like state.

"Professor, are you okay?" asked Devon.

"Is Vernon of sound mind?" Professor Stone asked, returning to his senses.

"I don't know?" Jess said. "He might be ill."

"Might explain some things," Professor Stone said, holding up Vernon's journal.

"That's not all. There's something in the lake," Jess said.

"Yeah, and whatever it is, it's big! It attacked us in the boathouse," Devon said.

Professor Stone stared reverently at Vernon's journal. "My God, the boy's done it."

***

Kate pounded on Professor Stone's door.

"Kate, what's wrong?" the professor said, letting her in.

"The lake is flooding from the levee break up at Madison. I'm afraid it won't be long before it reaches the trailers," Kate said, her heart beating faster than the wings of a hummingbird. She was unaccustomed to panic.

Where the hell were the kids?

"Kate, get on the phone. We need everyone over here. I'm afraid that this is going to be one helluva night!" Professor Stone said.

***

Professor Stone paced the floor preparing for what he had to say. It brought him back to those days behind the lectern, conjuring up a dazzling thought that might reside in his student's heads longer than the class period.

Jess and Devon sat at the kitchen table. Jasper and Claude had just arrived and were milling around impatiently, still unsure of why they were summoned. Kelly was still over at Kate's, waiting for Sean and Nell to show up.

Kate was on the phone. She waited for a moment then hung up the receiver.

"Liz still doesn't answer," she said.

"Probably took a sleeping pill and is dead to the world," Jasper said, shaking his head.

***

Liz bounced up and almost hit her head on the roof of the cab. She had not seen the speed bump in time to slow down. The golf cart's rear tires spun a few times on the wet pavement then held to the road.

The night sky was black as the inside of a coal bin. The persistent clouds kept the moon at bay and prevented it from shining through.

She was chilled from the rain. If she did not find Rosie soon, she would have to go back. Her hands ached trying to keep the wheel steady. Maybe Kate would help her search for Rosie. After all, it was Max's fault that her poor Rosie was out in this frightful weather.

Liz stopped the golf cart. She shined her flashlight on the *No Trespassing* sign on the chain-link fence at the edge of the turnaround. Reaching the end of the line, Liz was about to head back when she heard something whimpering from the other side of the fence.

Rosie, is that you?

CHAPTER FOURTEEN

Devon studied the professor, who was lost in his own thoughts, still clutching Vernon's journal as though he were holding the Holy Scripture.

"Should we get started?" Devon asked, impatiently.

"We called you all over to tell you that there is a crisis about to happen. Let me put it this way; all hell is about to let loose," Professor Stone said.

"What the hell are you talking about?" asked Jasper.

"Kate has just informed me that she believes that the trailer park is in danger of being flooded."

"Flooded?" Claude piped in.

"The levee up in Madison has ruptured, and the runoff is feeding into the lake. It won't be long before the lake rises up to the park," Kate told everyone.

"Then we better pack our valuables and get to high ground," Jasper said.

"That is the least of our worries," Professor Stone said.

"Losing our homes, all of our possessions, is the least of our worries," Jasper said, his face beginning to fluster.

"Let's not start a panic," Devon said, holding up his hands.

"Devon's right," Professor Stone said. "We need to remain calm."

"Before we go any further professor, I don't believe Jess has ever met Jasper and Claude," Devon said. "Jasper, Claude, this is Jess Murdock."

"It's a pleasure, Jess," Jasper said, extending his hand.

Jess exchanged a pumping handshake with Jasper and gave him a warm smile.

"Glad to meet you," Claude said, jumping down from the counter to shake her hand.

Devon could tell that Jasper and Claude were instantly taken with Jess.

"So, tell us about this bad news," Jasper said to Professor Stone.

"All right. Jess brought her brother's journal and asked me to read it. Vernon, a past biology student of mine, has been working on a particular project for the last four years. He was supposed to produce a prime aquaculture food source, one that could be harvested in abundance. It was meant to be a food source intended to put an end to world hunger."

"Sounds like a noble endeavor, but how does that propose a threat to us?" Claude asked.

"That is what I am about to tell you based upon what I was able to read. In the first fifty or so pages, his work seemed brilliant, despite the failures. After that, his writing seemed to drift, become incoherent at times. Most of the pages from that point on were ruined from water damage. It is from those that are still decipherable, that I was able to piece some of the puzzle together."

"And what might that be?" Devon asked.

"I'll get to that in a moment," Professor Stone said then continued by saying, "I hate to say this, Jess, but I suspect Vernon is suffering from delusions. Maybe even bordering into dementia."

Jess wished Professor Stone would just get on with it.

"Anyway, after a couple of years and many futile attempts, he finally made a breakthrough—a discovery that I found quite astonishing, almost unbelievable. Vernon had developed a process to incorporate key qualities of an entire family of species and meld them all into one, something that has never been done before. Only there was a problem," Professor Stone said.

"And what was that?" Jess asked.

"It no longer had to do with the project. Instead of harvesting a staple food source, he ended up breeding an integrated species that extended outside the normal and practical realm of aquaculture. By doing so, Vernon had managed to condense a million-year evolution process into a three-year span. To be more concise, Vernon has created a species more powerful and more deadly than any other marine creature on the planet."

"How can that be possible?" Jasper asked.

"We would have to ask Vernon. If I could see the program he was running on his computer—"

"All of his equipment was destroyed when the lab caught fire," Jess said.

"Well, then. With most of the pages of his journal ruined, I can only offer an educated guess."

"Come on, professor. Just get to the chase," Jasper said.

"Okay. To start, you must know that there are well over two thousand species of fish that fall into the category of *Siluriformes*," Professor Stone said.

"Would you mind translating that into layman terms?" Jasper asked.

"I'm sorry. I am referring to catfish."

"Get real, professor. Catfish?" Claude jabbed Jasper in the ribs.

"Yes, remarkable creatures. They range anywhere from European Wels that weigh over six hundred pounds to the minuscule candiru that are so small that they can evade a person's urinary tract.

"Siluriformes are the most unique of all species. That is probably why Vernon decided to use them for his experiment. He has inter-bred two silurid that he has named, Zeus and Athena. Are you familiar with these names?"

"Yeah, they're Greek gods, right?" Jasper said.

"That's right. Zeus is the god of thunder. That's what Vernon has named the male. Let me give you a demonstration," Stone said, and walked over to one of his aquariums.

"This is an electric catfish. Larger members of his family are capable of giving off three hundred and fifty volts of electricity. Listen." Professor Stone turned a switch on a small speaker that was beside the aquarium.

A crackling sound emitted from the speaker.

"Damn, professor, are you telling us that these things are electrically charged?" asked Jasper.

"Yes. A three-hundred-and-fifty-volt charge can stun a fish, even a human. An eight-foot electric eel can generate a charge of up to five hundred volts. That is enough to put down a horse. Judging by the current size of Vernon's creatures, they could easily generate five times that amount. That would be enough to easily kill an elephant. Who knows, maybe a herd of elephants."

"Claude almost drowned today. I bet one of these creatures had something to do with it," Jasper said.

"You really think so?" asked Claude.

"I'd bet money on it. Before you were pulled under, I went to pick up a dead fish out of the water and got the crap shocked out of me."

"Where was this?" Jess asked.

"Chickaree Creek."

"Devon and I had an encounter at the boathouse. But, we didn't get a good look at it," Jess told Jasper and Claude.

"That confirms it. They're here at the lake," Professor Stone said.

"What about the other one, Athena?" Devon asked.

"That, of course, is the female. Athena was known as the goddess of warfare, and aptly so. Both of these fish have a protective armor that covers most of their bodies. They have a keen sensory system that enables them to detect prey at phenomenal distances. And as they are still maturing, they have insatiable appetites. If these silurids were to invade the populace, by that I mean streams, lakes, even the oceans, they would destroy the balance of aquatic life as we know it."

"You said these things are still growing? What makes you think that?" Claude asked.

"One of Vernon's entries. Even though the fish are in a mature stage, they still continue to increase in mass."

"Professor. We saw growth markings at Vernon's lab. How big could these fish get?" asked Jess.

"Hard to say, twenty-five, thirty feet."

"That means they're bigger than a great white shark," Jasper said.

"Much larger. Great whites generally only get to twenty feet. These creatures are larger than the *Grampus orca*."

"Say, again," Devon asked.

"Killer whales," Professor Stone said. "They get up to twenty-six feet in length."

"So professor. What do you figure one of these fish weighs?" asked Jasper.

"These silurids would most doubt vary in size and weight being a male and female which is often the case in certain species. An educated guess would be somewhere in the range of five to six tons."

"Jesus, that's a damn big fish," Jasper said.

"I'll say," Claude said.

"There is something else that I should mention," Professor Stone said.

"Jesus, what else? Next, you're going to tell us that these damn things can breathe fire like a dragon," Jasper said with a grin.

"Hardly. But, they do have lungs, much like ours, and can spend short periods of time out of the water. In fact, they could probably—"

There was a loud thump at the door, which caused everyone to jump.

The front door opened, and Kelly came in, drenched from the rain.

She closed the door and froze once she saw everyone staring at her. "What?"

"Kelly, aren't Sean and Nell with you?" Kate asked.

"No. That's what I came over to tell you."

"We'll have to decide later what to do about these—silurids. Right now, we have to find my brother and sister," Devon said, jumping up from the table.

"Let's not forget about Vernon," Jess said.

"What? Your brother is here?" Devon asked.

"I believe so," she answered.

"I need to get some stuff from my trailer," Jasper said. "Claude and I will use my bass boat. We can cover more area that way."

"Professor, you and Jess better come with me. We'll take the Lake Patrol boat," Devon said.

"Kelly and I will check the trailer park," Kate said. "We might as well wake up Liz while we're at it."

Everyone scrambled for the door just as the lights went out.

"Damn, we've lost power!" Jasper yelled in the dark.

Someone fumbled in a kitchen drawer then clicked on a flashlight that shone on Kate. She had grabbed the phone and had the receiver pressed to her ear.

"That's not all," she said. "The phone's dead."

CHAPTER FIFTEEN

"I don't believe it," Sean said.

"What?" Nell asked, turning around in the bow seat.

"Look. The lights at the resort just went out."

It would be difficult getting back without the lights to guide them. Nell turned and peered out over the boat's bow.

"My arms are killing me," Sean said.

"I think I see something. It's Grizzly Island. I can see the old tree. And there's Max," she said, able to see her dog in the dim moonlight. Max sat patiently at the base of the tree.

"I can't believe he swam all the way out here," Sean said. He dipped the oars and leaned back.

"We're coming, boy, don't worry," Nell yelled.

Sean rowed vigorously toward the island.

Finally, the aluminum boat skimmed onto the sandy beach.

"You stay here, while I get Max," Sean said. He stood up and caught his foot on something and fell halfway out the boat.

"Man, what next?" Sean slipped his foot out of the strung bow with the quiver attached. He snatched up the bow-fishing rig and marched off toward the tree.

Nell watched anxiously as Sean walked away. She did not like being left alone in the boat, but as long as she could still see Sean, then she would be all right. Just as long as—

The moon disappeared behind a cloud, the night darker than the inside of a closed coffin.

"Sean. Sean! I'm scared," she called out. She couldn't see the tree now, even though it was only fifty feet away.

The stern of the boat rose up and a wave swept onto the beach.

Nell lost her balance and fell out onto the sand. She got up, brushed the wet sand from her pants. She knew it was best to stay put. If she wandered off and Sean could not find her, she would be in big trouble. And then she had a terrible thought.

She turned.

The boat was gone.

The moon broke from the cloud cover for a brief moment.

She could see the boat drifting out onto the lake in too deep of water for her to retrieve. Sean was going to go ballistic. *Didn't I say to stay in the boat! Now, we'll never get home!*

The boat disappeared into the night.

"What do I do now?" Nell said, wanting to cry.

She saw a dark shape coming toward the island.

As she watched, praying that it was the boat drifting back, she suddenly realized it was much too big. She rubbed her eyes, took another look, but still couldn't believe what she was seeing.

A giant fish emerged out of the water.

Nell took a few steps backward.

The fish moved onto the shore on its belly. It looked down at her with cold, black eyes then opened its mouth—which was large enough to gulp down a cow—and released an eerie gasp.

Nell stood still, her feet frozen to the ground.

The fish looked like a humongous catfish but different. Unlike a catfish that had smooth skin, this fish was covered with large octagon-like plates—not scales—resembling large stepping stones. Its ribcage was pronounced and sleek—a design that made the fish appear to be a fast swimmer. All the catfish Nell remembered had flatter bodies, as they were bottom feeders. This fish had a high-ridged back.

It had eight whiskers like a catfish, except these were six feet in length. The large whiskers flitted about, caressing the wet sand.

Nell realized the whiskers were searching for something.

Searching for her!

The fish slithered over the sand, stopped, then tucked its front fins under its body. It pushed its chest up, supporting itself under its fins and towered over Nell.

It stood taller than their trailer.

Slowly, the fished *walked* toward her.

"SEAN!" she screamed.

Nell turned and ran blindly in the darkness until she collided into Sean.

"I thought I told you to stay with the boat," Sean snapped, standing at the base of the tree, holding Max by the collar.

"It's a giant walking fish and it's coming this way," Nell shouted.

"There's no such thing," Sean said.

"Look for yourself," Nell said, hiding behind Sean.

"You can't be serious," Sean said, once he saw the fish.

"Believe me now?"

"Get back!"

Max broke free and charged the fish. He stopped short of the fish, barking and snarling. The fish glanced down and lunged for the dog.

Brave, but not entirely stupid, Max reared back on his haunches and dodged the fish then came back for another assault.

Irritated by the persistent dog, the fish jerked back with the shaft-like appendage behind its front fin.

Max ducked as it swept over his head.

"Get out of there, Max," Sean yelled. "Nell, up the tree! Come on, I'll help you."

Sean picked her up so that she could grab onto the lowest branch. She used her feet and pushed herself up. Sean was right behind her. They kept climbing until they were almost twenty feet above the ground. It was another ten feet up to the top of the tree.

"We'll be safe up here," Sean said.

"Maybe you can scare the fish off with that," Nell said, pointing at Sean's bow.

"I'll do better than that," Sean said, pulling an arrow out of the quiver. He inserted the base of the arrow in the bowstring. He pulled back, aimed, and released.

The arrow flew straight for the fish's head, but instead of burrowing into the fish's flesh, the arrow only glanced off the hard shell and fell to the sand.

"What the—?" Sean plucked another arrow from the quiver and took another shot.

Again, the arrow was unable to penetrate the fish.

"This thing is like a Brinks truck," Sean said.

The fish lumbered toward the base of the tree.

Max came from behind. Sensing the dog, the fish cocked its tail to one side and came back with a powerful swipe, narrowly missing Max. He turned tail and scampered away.

"MAX!" Nell yelled.

The fish began to push itself up the trunk of the tree.

"It's okay, Nell. We're safe up here."

Nell yelled when she lost her balance. She grabbed for a branch but missed and fell.

The fish was directly below.

Sean reached out and snagged the strap on her life vest. Nell dangled in the air while Sean held on.

The fish looked up and opened its gaping maw.

"Don't let it eat me," Nell pleaded with her brother.

"It's not eating anyone," Sean said, pulling her up.

The oak's roots sucked out of the mud, the weight of the heavy fish too much for the old tree to bear.

CHAPTER SIXTEEN

"I checked the rental boats. There's a boat missing," Jasper said, bouncing down the boat docks. Claude was right behind.

"Then they must be out on the lake," Devon said. He was standing at the helm of the 17-foot Whaler used for patrolling the lake. Professor Stone and Jess were also onboard.

"What do you have there?" Devon called out.

"If these things are as dangerous as the professor says they are, we're going to need some fire power," Jasper said, raising a shotgun over his head.

"Jasper, you know the rules. No firearms in the resort."

"What would you suggest? Bring our poles?"

"Okay, just be careful. Sean and Nell are out there."

Jasper and Claude climbed down into Jasper's bass boat moored next to the Whaler.

Claude sat down in the passenger seat, while Jasper got behind the steering wheel.

Jasper fired up the 150-horse power outboard motor. Claude plugged in the cord for the portable spotlight.

Slowly, both boats backed out of their berths then turned to face out toward the flat water of the lake.

Devon switched on the navigation lights and the bright halogen searchlight.

The boats roared off, bouncing over the water until they both leveled out. They rode alongside each other, increasing their speed. At forty miles per hour, both boats peeled away from each other in different directions like a well-executed aquatic stunt.

***

The rain pelted Nell and Sean, struggling to stay in the tree.

"Did you see that?" Sean said, holding onto Nell.

"See what?"

"I thought I saw lights on the other side of the lake."

"No, I didn't see anything," Nell said.

"They must know we're out here and are looking for us. It won't be long now," Sean said.

That's when the tree shuddered and toppled over.

Sean and Nell clung on like two ticks on a dog as the tree crashed into the water. Gradually, the branches began to sink, and the water rose above their feet.

The fish moved up the trunk of the tree, pushing its head through the branches, breaking them off. It shoved its way in closer and closer.

"Sean, what do we do?"

"I don't know, just keep backing up."

"Where? There's nowhere to go." They were already to the top branches of the tree. Beyond was nothing but water.

The fished opened its cavernous mouth, expelling a sour smell. Then it let out a gurgling gasp so frightening that Nell screamed.

The tree began to sink, dipping further into the water.

The fish continued to smash through the branches.

"Get in, quick!" a voice called out.

Nell turned and saw a man in a rubber raft appear out of the dark.

"I suggest you hurry," the stranger said.

Sean held onto Nell. She reached out for the man's hand. She was quickly swept onboard. Sean jumped in after her.

The fish made a wild attempt to get at them, but was caught in the thick, gnarled branches.

The man pushed the start button, throttled the handle on the small outboard, and cut an evasive course to clear the tree limbs.

"Thanks for getting us out of there," Sean said.

"It's the least I can do," the man replied.

"I'm Sean. This is my sister, Nell."

"Please to make your acquaintance. My name is Vernon. Vernon Murdock."

"Where did that thing come from?" asked Sean.

"That's a long story. Right now, I suggest we get moving. I don't think that tree will hold him off for long," Vernon said, speeding up. He kept glancing down at a black box at his feet.

Nell could see a tiny screen lit up with two red dots inside of green squiggly lines.

"We forgot Max!" Nell shouted.

"He's right here by my feet. He's a little banged up, but he'll live," Vernon said.

Nell had been so busy watching the fish that she had not bothered to look down. Though Max was extremely tired from his ordeal, he still managed a few wags of his tail when he looked up at Nell.

"I'm glad to see you, too, Max," Nell said, and hugged his neck.

The outboard motor suddenly reduced power.

Nell looked over at Vernon. His hand had slipped off the throttle, and he was beginning to slump over.

"Mr. Murdock! Are you okay?" she asked.

Vernon abruptly sat back up. "Just felt a little light-headed for a moment. I'm fine. Where's home?"

"It's that way, I think," Nell said, pointing out into the darkness.

Vernon steered the raft in the direction of Nell's finger.

***

"Sean, Nell," Kelly shouted. She swept her flashlight from one trailer to the other.

"Let's check on Liz," Kate said when they came to the Fallow trailer.

Most of the windmills had blown down from the storm. The flowerbeds were flattened from the heavy rain.

Kate knocked on the door. There was no answer.

"She probably can't hear us," Kelly shouted to be heard over the deafening rain.

"We better check on her." Kate grabbed the doorknob, gave it a twist, and the door opened.

"Mrs. Fallow, it's Kelly and Kate," Kelly said.

"Rosie would be barking up a storm by now. Something's not right," Kate said.

They ventured inside, shining their flashlights, careful not to trip over the furniture. Everything looked normal. They went back to the bedroom.

The bed was still made. Liz and Rosie were not home.

"I don't like this," Kate said.

They went outside and looked around.

Parked beside the trailer was Liz's vintage Studebaker. Kelly wiped the driver's window and peered inside. Nothing.

"Over here," Kate said.

"Did you find something?" Kelly asked, rushing to the other side of the trailer.

"Liz's golf cart. It's gone."

"You don't think she is out in this storm, do you?"

"I don't know. Come on, we'll take the truck."

They ran back to Kate's trailer. Kate darted inside to get the keys while Kelly got in the truck. It was already 1:30. She was worn out.

What was happening?

First, Sean and Nell go missing, and now, Mrs. Fallow.

Kelly was so tired that her body involuntarily jerked to the rhythm of the rain pounding on the cab.

***

"Do you even have any idea where we are?" asked Victoria, wedged between Bernie and Tony in the front seat. They were parked under an Interstate 5 freeway overpass.

"No, not really," Bernie replied.

Most of the evening had been wasted summoning the road service, getting towed to a gas station, and having the tire repaired. Afterward, they had searched for Lake Recluse. The topography map had been useless for directions, as it didn't show roads or major highways.

"What now?" Tony asked.

The rain cascaded like a waterfall over the edge of the overpass.

Just then a horn blared and headlight beams crisscrossed out into the night.

They heard a loud crash and tires screeching on the freeway above, along with a horrific explosion of crunching metal and shattering glass.

A body soared down and splattered on the roadway in front of the van.

"Holy shit!" Bernie yelled. He hit the high beams. The light shined on a man spread eagle on the asphalt, his face mashed to pulp.

"Jesus, his face looks like rhubarb pie," Tony said.

"Don't," Victoria said, hand over her mouth, about to throw up on the dashboard.

"You okay?" Tony asked.

"Hey, we're in luck," Bernie said, and pointed.

Victoria gazed beyond the body and saw a sign: Lake Recluse.

"Thank God. Go!" she pleaded.

"Whoa. What about him?" Tony nodded at the man lying on the road.

"There's nothing we can do for him, he's dead," Victoria said.

"Maybe there's someone hurt up on the freeway."

Already they could hear sirens in the distance.

"That's the CHP. We hang around they'll end up detaining us for hours, asking silly questions. Besides, there's no story here. We need to get to Lake Recluse. Now, move it, before they spot us!"

Bernie gave the body a wide berth then sped off down the road.

***

When CHP officers Rick Stokes and Ken Redfield pulled up in their cruiser, the tires on the overturned car on the grassy freeway divider were still spinning.

Another car had plowed into the guardrail.

They got out, leaving the emergency lights flashing. Both officers were wearing yellow raincoats and carrying flashlights. They split up to assist the distressed motorists.

Stokes ran over to the driver's door of the overturned vehicle and shined his flashlight inside. A woman driver was suspended upside down by her seatbelt. He banged on the window. The woman was either unconscious or dead. At this point, he wasn't sure which.

He went over to the other side of the car and smashed out the passenger window.

"Lady, can you hear me?" he asked, crawling inside. There was no response.

He had already summoned assistance, so he knew it would only be a matter of minutes before the paramedic team showed up. He decided it was best not to move her. As he backed out, he noticed blood dripping down from the car seat onto the headliner.

"Hey, Rick!" Redfield shouted from the guardrail next to the other car.

"What?"

"The driver took a nosedive straight out the windshield. He's down there."

"Poor sucker." Stokes shook his head, thinking that's what happens when you don't wear your seatbelt, thankful that the woman had had the foresight to wear hers.

Redfield stepped over the guardrail and disappeared down the embankment.

The woman stirred and let out a tiny murmur.

"Don't worry, we'll have you out of there before you know it," Stokes said.

As if on cue, the paramedic van pulled up. Two paramedics jumped out carrying their emergency kits and rushed over to Stokes.

"In here. A woman. I think she's bleeding," he told them and stepped out of the way.

While the paramedics did their job, Stokes began accessing the accident scene for his report. The left side of the car against the guardrail and the right side of the woman's car were both crinkled, suggesting that they had collided, slamming into each other. After the impact, the one car had veered off, smashing into the guardrail, and the woman's car had spun out of control and flipped over. He would pace off the skid marks later to calculate how fast the drivers had been going before the accident.

Stokes was watching the paramedics. They struggled to free the woman from her seat belt. He noticed a hole in the passenger door just below the door handle. He took a closer look. The hole was big enough that he could fit his finger inside.

He strode over to the other car impaled on the guardrail. He leaned in through the driver's opened window.

"I put a tarp over the body and set up some flares," Redfield said, climbing back over the guardrail.

"Well, well. What do we have here?" Stokes said, moving back out of the car. He was dangling a Smith and Wesson .357 Magnum by the trigger guard with his pen.

"Don't tell me that stiff down there is the Highway Marauder." Redfield grinned.

"Talk about justice."

"I'll say. Better spruce up, we're going to be on the news."

CHAPTER SEVENTEEN

Claude swept the shore with the spotlight. So far, they had come up dry. He couldn't help thinking of what would happen if Sean and Nell were to meet up with one of those fish. What'd the professor call them? Oh yeah, *silurid.* He sure hoped to hell the kids were safe.

"You mind not pointing that thing this way," he said.

"Quit your worrying," Jasper replied, resting the shotgun across his lap.

"Easy for you to say."

"Don't tell me you're all spooked because of a couple of stupid fish."

"You heard the professor. He said they were armor-plated."

"Yeah, well, this is an Ithaca Mag-10 Roadblocker, guaranteed to put a chink in that thick hide of theirs."

"Yeah, well, do me a favor and keep it pointed the other way."

"Hey, we play our cards right, we might have to buy us up some freezers once we kill those giant catfish."

"There you go, always thinking of that gut of yours."

"A man has to eat."

"Don't forget why we're really out here."

"Hell, those things harm a hair on Sean or Nell, I'll hunt them down to my last dying breath."

Something slammed into the boat's bow.

"What was that?" Claude said. His nerves were as ragged as Jasper's skivvies.

"Shine the light over there," Jasper said.

Claude directed the spotlight on some floating debris.

"Must be from the storm."

Claude panned the light over the bank of Adobe Creek. The creek was no longer dried up but alive and turbulent.

"What's that?" Jasper asked.

"Where?"

"Over there," Jasper said, pointing farther down the shore.

Jasper slowed down, cut the engine, then hit the tilt switch. The bow of the bass boat nudged onto the beach.

"Looks like a campsite," Jasper said, stepping from the boat.

Claude got out. He took a flashlight out of his coat pocket and switched it on.

"The campfire is still warm," Jasper said, holding his hand over the coals.

"Good God, will you look at that," Claude said, shining his flashlight into the woods.

"Damn. Talk about driving your rig into the ground," Jasper said.

Claude walked over to the wrecked truck. The windshield had been smashed out and was on the ground. He tried opening the driver's door, but it was jammed shut. He reached through where the windshield had been and pulled down the visor, shining the light on the registration.

"Well, what do you know," he said

"What?" Jasper asked.

"The truck belongs to Vernon Murdock."

* * *

"You're chilled to the bone," Kate said, helping Kelly out of the truck and up to the trailer.

"Kate, I'm okay, really."

"Nonsense. There's enough going on without you catching pneumonia."

They went inside, and Kate guided the girl to the couch.

"We better get you out of these wet things," Kate said, and removed Kelly's jacket.

While Kelly undressed, Kate got the girl some clothes. She went into the kitchen and came back with a lit kerosene lamp.

"Don't want you tripping in the dark," she said.

"Kate, I feel so bad," Kelly said, lying under a comforter.

"I know you do."

"No! I mean I want to help."

"You're not going to be much help if you're sick. You just rest."

"I hope you find them."

"You and me both."

Kate went out the door and down to the truck. She jumped in and turned the ignition key. The solenoid clicked twice, but the starter refused to turn over the engine. She turned the key again. Nothing.

"Not now!" Kate yelled. She grabbed the steering wheel with both hands and shook the living shit out of it. Not believing her luck, she laid her head down on the steering wheel. Of all the times for the truck to fail her, it had to be at the most crucial moment. She was about to burst into tears when a thought crossed her mind.

"Jess's Bronco," Kate said aloud. She charged out of the cab and ran down the road. She cut down a path that led between two trailers and came out at Jonathan's mobile home.

"Please be there," she said, grabbing the door handle of the Bronco. The door opened. She peered inside and saw the keys dangling from the ignition.

"Thank you," Kate said and jumped into the vehicle. She started the engine and drove off in search of Liz.

***

"They could be anywhere," Devon said, steering the Whaler out of Landon Cove.

"We'll find them," Jess assured him.

"Maybe we should head further up," Professor Stone said.

"There's nothing up there, but the dam. I doubt very seriously if they could have gone that far."

"Then, where are they?" Jess asked.

"Hell, I don't know. Maybe you're right. We'll check the dam," Devon said.

***

Jasper pushed the bass boat out into the water and jumped in. He tilted the prop back down into the water, started the engine, and turned the bow around.

"I'll bet you anything those kids are snug in their beds right about now, while we're out here freezing our tails off. What do you think?" Jasper asked.

"Don't count on it."

The hull skimmed over the lake like a flat polished stone.

"Man, I love running at night," Jasper said, giving the bass boat more power.

"Just don't get us killed," Claude said. He shifted in his seat and shined the spotlight over the outboard motor. He could see the white water of the boat's wake beyond the stern.

The white water parted in the middle as a dark mass sliced up to the surface.

"Oh, shit almighty."

"I know, isn't this a rush?" Jasper said.

"No! Behind us!"

Jasper spun around and looked over his shoulder. "Oh jeez!"

The fish was keeping pace with the bass boat.

"Faster!" Claude screamed.

Jasper shoved the throttle all the way down.

The vibrating outboard motor roared, threatening to rip itself off the transom.

"It's gaining," Claude yelled, shining the beam on the fish's back. The thing was as big as three bass boats strung together. He reached down and grabbed the shotgun.

Claude aimed at the fish and pulled the trigger. The barrel lit up as the shotgun bucked in his hands. The payload struck the surface of the water just short of the fish.

He ratcheted another shell into the chamber.

"Shine that light up ahead, I can't see where the hell I'm going," Jasper yelled.

Before Claude could react, the boat surged upward, throwing off his aim, and the shotgun went off, blasting the engine cover apart on the outboard motor.

"Ah, shit!"

Jasper looked back and saw the blown-up engine. "Jesus, Claude. What the hell did you do?"

The outboard motor coughed smoke, sputtered, and died.

***

"Devon, did you hear that? Sounded like shots," Jess said.

"Must be Jasper and Claude," Devon said. He cranked the helm to the left and opened up the Whaler. The boat vaulted across the lake like a snowmobile slamming across a field of moguls.

Jess and Stone shifted forward to help trim the fast-moving boat.

"I see their boat," Jess shouted.

"Where's Jasper and Claude?" Devon asked, tracking the beam of the Whaler's searchlight on the bass boat.

Devon slowed the Whaler and maneuvered it alongside the other boat.

Suddenly, Jasper and Claude stood up.

"You got to get us out of here!" Jasper yelled.

"Hurry, climb aboard," Professor Stone said. He extended a long-shaft boat hook for Jasper to grab a hold of.

Jasper handed the shotgun up to Jess and then grabbed the wooden shaft of the boat hook above the shank. He placed his other hand on the Whaler's railing and began to pull himself up.

The bass boat was punched out of the water, and Claude was thrown out.

Jasper released the boat hook and clung to the railing with both hands, drumming his feet on the Whaler's hull.

Coming back down, the bass boat crashed into the rear starboard section of the Whaler's gunwale, crushing and snapping laminated Fiberglas chunks and leaving a gaping-wide hole in the side of the boat.

The lake gushed into the ruptured vessel.

"Professor, pull me up, pull me up," Jasper screamed.

The silurid lunged out of the water and belly-flopped on the bass boat taking it to the bottom of the lake.

Professor Stone could not believe what he had just witnessed. It was like watching a whale destroy a dingy.

He reached down and grabbed Jasper by the scruff and pulled him aboard.

A pointed bone-like shaft poked through the Fiberglas.

"What the hell is that?" Devon yelled.

"A spine from behind its pectoral fin. Watch out, it's venomous," Professor Stone warned.

The spine pulled out. Rammed in again, this time, stabbing Jasper in the leg, gashing open his calf. Jasper screamed. Blood gushed on the deck.

"Devon, I see Claude," Jess yelled, pointing at the water.

Devon ran over, snatched up the boat hook, and leaned over the side.

Claude was fighting to stay afloat. His head and shoulders jerked as though he were suffering a seizure.

"Grab hold," Devon yelled.

Claude's mouth opened in a silent scream, the air around him crackling off the lake's surface. He flailed one last time and went under.

"Claude!" Devon waited, but the man never came up.

Jasper had passed out on the deck.

"Jess! Take the helm. Get us the hell out of here!" Devon yelled.

"We're sinking!" she replied.

"No, we're not. The Whaler's designed to stay afloat even if the hull is punctured. Come on, get us out of here!"

Jess gunned the badly damaged Whaler and steered for the marina.

Professor Stone knelt over Jasper and applied pressure to the gash on the injured man's leg.

"Jasper's lost a lot of blood," Professor Stone said, elevating the leg.

"He's going to die if we don't get him to a hospital," Jess said.

Everyone fell silent as the Whaler limped across the lake.

CHAPTER EIGHTEEN

Kate had spent the best part of an hour combing the resort for her friend. She had driven around the trailer park, checked the campgrounds, and a few of the beach areas, but Liz was nowhere to be found.

Her spirits lifted when she came to the turnaround at the dam site and found Liz's pink golf cart abandoned next to the chain-link fence.

Kate stopped the Bronco, turned off the ignition, but left the headlights on. She climbed out of the vehicle and pulled up her hood to ward off the rain.

Switching on her flashlight, Kate inspected the fence line. She spotted a hole just under the fence, big enough for someone to crawl through. The furrow was muddy with standing water. A tattered strip of pink cloth had caught on the jagged edge of the fence.

"Liz," Kate muttered. "Liz! Liz, are you out there?" she yelled.

Kate did not care to crawl through the mud to get to the other side of the fence. She knew she could scale the fence, but then when she found Liz, it would be a chore, if not impossible, to boost Liz over the fence. There had to be a better way.

A steady runoff of rainwater streamed under the fence onto the turnaround. That meant the ground was saturated. It also meant that the posts holding up the fence were not solidly anchored, that she might be able to force the fence over.

She glanced over at the Bronco. A heavy-duty brush guard was mounted over the grill.

Kate went back to the truck and got inside. She started the Bronco, put the transmission into reverse, and backed up. Once she felt she had enough running distance, she shifted into drive, pushed the accelerator pedal to the floor, and charged the fence.

The chain-link fence gave way to the impact, the bulldozing Bronco flattening the barrier to the ground.

Kate went in another fifty feet before stopping. She switched off the ignition, again leaving the headlights on. She got out, walked around the front of the vehicle, and looked up the embankment that led to the first cave.

She dug her boots into the slippery slope and climbed up.

Reaching the mouth of the cave, she shined her flashlight inside. The cavern stretched back about forty feet. She could hear seepage draining down the interior walls.

"Liz! Are you in there?"

There was no answer.

She decided to check the other cave.

Kate was just entering the next cave when her flashlight flickered and went out.

"Not now," she protested.

She slapped the flashlight in the palm of her hand and it went back on.

"Liz! Can you hear me?"

"Kate! We're in here!"

"Oh, thank God." Kate continued inside the cave. She tread quietly, panning the light along one wall then the other. Ten feet ahead, and to the left, was a narrow passage, large enough for a person to crawl into.

"For God's sake, Kate! Get in here!" Liz shouted.

Kate ran over to the grotto and shined the light inside.

Liz and Rose were huddled twenty feet back at the rear of the chamber.

"Kate, hurry, get in here," Liz pleaded.

"Yeah, but don't you want to—?"

"Quit arguing!"

Kate hunkered down and crawled into the passage.

"Liz, what happened to you?" Kate said, once she had reached her friend.

Liz's hair and face were caked with mud. Her jacket was grayish-brown with a few specks of pink.

"I know. I must look a fright," Liz said.

"What in the world are you doing in here?"

"Finding my Rosie." Rosie was on Liz's lap and looked petrified.

"Well, I'm getting you out of here."

"No! We can't go out there," Liz said.

"You'll catch your death if you stay in here."

"There are worse things to fear, trust me."

Kate's flashlight flickered and went out. "I knew I shouldn't have bought these bargain brand batteries." She slapped the flashlight and the light came back on.

"The truck is just right outside," she said. "You'll see the headlights when we go out."

Again, the flashlight faltered and went out.

Rosie let out a menacing growl.

"Shhh. Be still," Liz said. "It's coming back."

"What's coming back?" Kate looked through the passage and could see a faint glow from the Bronco's headlights filtering into the cave.

An immense shadow reflected off the far wall. She heard a loud scuffling noise, like something of great bulk dragging itself across the floor of the cave.

And that is when she saw the huge fin step in front of the passage entry.

"Oh Kate," Liz whispered, clutching Kate's arm.

"That is why you were afraid to leave."

The creature pulled itself along on its belly.

"It's been coming in and out of here all night."

"Sooner, or later, we've got to get out of here."

The light flickered out for a moment and came back on, shining on a gigantic tail passing by.

"Tell me I'm losing my mind," Liz said. "And that's not real."

"I'm afraid it's real all right."

And with that, Rosie began to whimper.

***

Kelly's body ached right down to her toes. She curled up on the couch and pulled the comforter over her shoulders.

"Kelly?"

Kelly opened her eyes, and when she looked up, there was Nell and Sean standing next to the couch.

"Where have you two been? Everyone's looking all over for you guys."

"We were looking for Max," Nell replied, and gave her brother a strange look. Kelly sensed a conspiracy, but before she could question them, Nell went on by saying, "We almost got eaten by a giant fish. It chased us up a tree and everything. Even knocked the tree down. Good thing Mr. Murdock was there to save us."

"You can do better than that," Kelly said. She had conjured up some fibs in her time, but this one was lame as a one-legged dog.

"It happened just like Nell said," Sean said.

"Oh, yeah. So, where is this Mr. Murdock then?" Kelly sat up on the couch.

The wick had dried out in the kerosene lamp so the room was dark.

"He's sitting right there," Nell said, pointing to a shadow in the corner of the room.

Just then, the front door flew open.

Devon and Professor Stone carried Jasper in and put the semi-conscious man on the couch.

"My leg's on fire," Jasper groaned.

"Kelly, we need some more blankets," Professor Stone said.

Kelly ran back to the hall closet and came back with an armful of blankets. She covered Jasper. "Wasn't Claude with you all?" she asked.

"Claude's dead."

"Oh, my God."

Devon looked across the room and saw his sister and brother. "Where the hell have you two been?" he snapped.

"Max was lost. We went to find him," Nell said.

Devon looked in the kitchen and saw Max sprawled on the floor, his head tucked down between his front paws, looking guilty as sin.

"Is that what happened?" Devon asked again, this time directing his question at Sean.

"What, you think we're making it up?" Sean snapped back.

"Kelly, turn up that lamp," Devon said.

Kelly dipped the wick back into the kerosene then turned up the key. Soon, the room brightened, and she could see a man sitting in the recliner, calm and collective as though he were a forgotten guest.

"Vernon!" Jess said.

"Jess," he replied.

"How did you get in here?" Devon asked.

"Vernon saved us," Sean said.

"What?"

"There was this gigantic fish. I never saw anything like it. Vernon rescued us with his raft."

"Yeah, well, you wouldn't have been in danger if it wasn't for him," Devon said, glaring at Vernon, who didn't seem phased in the very least.

Kelly thought it strange that Vernon could just sit, cool as a cucumber, even though he was sweating profusely like the temperature was a hundred degrees. She couldn't stop shivering she was so cold.

"There's no point fighting about that now," Professor Stone said.

"The professor is right. We need to get Jasper medical attention," Jess said.

"The sooner the better. We'll need to keep an eye on Jasper's leg. That barb was venomous. His leg could easily become infected, even go gangrene," Professor Stone said.

"How are we going to get Jasper out of here if the road is closed?" Jess asked.

"We'll figure a way," Devon said.

Kelly's head was spinning.

"Whoa. You mean Nell and Sean are telling the truth?" she asked.

"Yep. These two are lucky to be alive," Devon said. "Aren't we forgetting something?"

"What?" Professor Stone asked.

"Those fish, the silurids."

"What about them? This is a lake. They're not going anywhere," Professor Stone replied.

"That's where you're wrong. The lake is rising fast. Pretty soon, it will be up to the mouth of the diversion tunnel at the dam. That tunnel was meant to channel water from the lake into the Sacramento River. If those things get out through that tunnel, there's no telling where they'll end up," Devon said.

"I hadn't thought of that," Professor Stone said.

"As I see it, we have only two choices. Get help or stop them ourselves."

"Vernon, we need your help," Jess said, and knelt beside the recliner. "How do we stop them?"

"I don't know," Vernon replied.

"Come on, Vernon. Tell us how we can kill them!" Devon said.

"You can't. I won't let you."

"Vernon, don't you see what you've done? Don't you realize what these creatures could do to our eco-system?" Professor Stone said.

Vernon fell silent.

Jess placed her hand on Vernon's forehead. "He's burning up!"

"He might have pneumonia," Professor Stone said.

"Vernon, you're bleeding," Jess said after she removed her hand from Vernon's head and saw the blood.

"I hit my head pretty hard when I crashed the truck," Vernon said. He leaned back in the recliner like a traveler exhausted after a long journey.

Jasper groaned on the couch.

Devon glanced about the room. "Wait a minute. Where's my mom?"

"She went looking for Liz," Kelly said.

"She did what?"

CHAPTER NINETEEN

After making Jasper as comfortable as possible, Devon and Professor Stone helped Vernon into Kate's bedroom and put him on the bed where Jess dressed her brother's head wound. Vernon quickly drifted off to sleep.

Everyone congregated around the kitchen table cluttered with mail, some school supplies, one of Nell's textbooks, and a kerosene lamp.

"Anyone have any ideas what we should do?" Professor Stone asked.

Devon absentmindedly picked up a pencil and began to nervously tap it on the tabletop.

"I know there's a road crew working up near the main road. Should be there just after dawn. One of us could hike up there and get help," Jess said.

"Be tough in this weather, but it may be our only chance," Devon said, still tapping the pencil.

"I'll go," Sean said. "I can use the golf cart then hoof it the rest of the way."

"No, you better let me," Devon said.

"I can do it. Besides, don't you have to go look for Mom?"

"Sean's right. We need you here, Devon," Jess said. "Let Sean go."

"All right."

"Well, now that we have decided on that, we still have those fish to worry about," Professor Stone said.

Nell came into the kitchen carrying a small black box.

"What do you have there?" Jess asked.

"I don't know. It's Vernon's."

"May I see it?" asked Professor Stone.

Nell gave him the box.

Professor Stone lifted the lid and examined the contraption. "It's a tracking device."

"You don't think Vernon was using that device to keep tabs on the silurids, do you?" asked Devon.

"Maybe." Professor Stone flicked on a switch and a greenish glow shone on his face. "I'll be. It's configured to the shoreline around the lake. These two red dots must be Zeus and Athena."

Everyone leaned in to see the screen.

"Judging by this, they are somewhere around the southern part of the lake."

"Okay, so we know where they are. Now what?" Devon asked.

"Let's think for a minute. We know due to their abnormal size that they must possess extraordinary keen sensory abilities, both gustatory and auditory," Jess said.

"Say again?" Devon said, rapping the pencil on the table.

"Catfish possess the ability to actually taste a food source through their skin, as well as having hypersensitive senses. These silurids could probably hear a minnow swimming, halfway across the lake. They rely on their instincts, reflexes, not their brains. We just need a way to lure them into a trap."

"Devon, you mind putting that pencil down. It's hard enough to think without you doing that," Professor Stone said.

"That's it!" Jess said.

"What?" Devon said, tossing the pencil on the table.

"In Europe, fishermen use a technique called klonking. They hollow out this shaft of wood about the length of your forearm then by using a paddling motion on the surface are actually able to attract fish to their bait. We could use a similar method."

"Baiting them is one thing, hooking them is another," Devon said.

"I may have the hook," Jasper said, balancing on his good leg at the kitchen's threshold.

Devon jumped up and helped Jasper to a chair.

"There's...RDX in my trailer," Jasper said, wheezing out the words.

"What's RDX?" asked Professor Stone.

"Plastic explosive. Used to work demolition years ago."

"You mean to tell me you have explosives in your trailer?" Devon asked.

"Sorry, Devon. For violating another one of your trailer park rules," Jasper said.

"I don't believe it," Devon said in an exasperated tone.

"Don't get sore. You guys are family to me," Jasper said and hung his head. "So was Claude."

"Tell us more about this RDX," Devon said.

"I've worked with all kinds of explosives. Dynamite. Nitroglycerin. Lost most of my hand and got this scar from nitro. RDX is more stable, not volatile like TNT. No fuse, just takes an electrical charge, and BOOM!" Jasper clapped his hands together to simulate an explosion.

He leaned forward on the table. The flickering light from the kerosene lamp accentuated his solemn mood.

"Devon. RDX is a serious explosive. You make a mistake and there is no correcting it. Don't ever forget that. And whatever you do, don't violate rule number one."

"What is rule number one?"

"Always finish the job with the same number of digits you started with," Jasper said, stroking his scarred cheek with the remaining fingers on his crippled hand.

"Sounds like solid advice. Now tell us what we need to know," Devon said.

For the next few minutes, Jasper explained how the RDX was to be rigged and had just finished telling them how to set the timer when he gasped.

"Jasper!" Devon reached out but not in time to catch Jasper. He slipped off the chair and fell to the floor.

"Oh, my God!" Jess screamed.

Jasper lay motionless, dead.

"Look at his pant leg," Stone said.

Devon grabbed a knife from the kitchen counter and sliced along the outer seam of Jasper's trousers. "Ah jeez!"

Jasper's leg had turned a dark purple and was swollen twice what it should be. Minute beads of green pus oozed out of every pore.

***

Tony had turned off the dispatch radio in case they received a call to return to the station. If anyone should ask, he was going to say that they had blown a fuse. He even had a blown fuse handy to replace the good one, in the event someone became suspicious and wanted to verify his story.

"We should call it a night. I'm tired of driving," Bernie said.

"We're almost there," Victoria said.

"Think so, eh?" Bernie stopped the van.

Ahead were five sawhorses lined up and blocking the road. A *Road Closed Mudslide* sign was attached to the middle sawhorse.

"I guess you got your wish," Tony said to Bernie.

"I'm not giving up," Victoria said.

"Then what do you suggest?"

Victoria thought for a moment. "I got it. Miles Forbes."

"The joker that flies the chopper for traffic," said Tony.

"He's always had a thing for me. Frankly, I can't stand the jerk. But, I think I can convince him to fly us out to that lake."

"And how are you going to do that?"

"I'll call him."

"At four in the morning?"

"Like I said, the guy has a hard-on for me. What can I say?" Victoria pushed the appropriate buttons on her cell phone and put the phone to her ear. A few seconds passed.

"Miles? Morning, I didn't wake you did I?" Victoria purred. "What? I did. I thought you would be on your way to work. No! It's your day off. Damn. Oh, no honey, I mean damn I was hoping to see you at the station. I'm sorry, too. Dinner? You want to invite me to dinner tonight? Well, that sounds fantastic, but I'm sort of in a bind. What sort of bind?

"The station is expecting me to cover this hot exclusive, but my crew and I can't get there as the road is closed. Mudslide. Yes, it is very important. Could you help us? I know it's your day off, but don't you think you could, maybe borrow a helicopter. I know that sounds silly. You can!" Victoria put her hand over the phone. "He fell for it," she said to Tony and Bernie.

"What a horn dog," Tony said.

Victoria elbowed Tony then went on to say into the phone, "Really, honey you're a sweetie. Where? Give us an hour to find a place for you to land, and I'll call you and tell you where we are. I'm looking forward to dinner. Yes. Me, too." Victoria closed the phone. "The things I have to do to get a story."

Bernie found a wide enough spot in the road and turned the van around.

CHAPTER TWENTY

Jess held the boathouse door open for Devon. He carried in the red, metal box that they had taken from Jasper's trailer. He set the box down on the workbench.

Worried that the Whaler might flounder if another storm struck, Devon berthed the boat in the slip. The hull rubbed against the wood sides of the slip, screeching like fingernails drawn down a chalkboard.

"So what is this harebrained plan again?" Professor Stone said, closing the door behind him.

"We rig the Whaler with the plastic explosive. I lure the fish to the boat, and you blow it up. And no more fish. Problem solved," Devon said.

"Devon, remember what Jasper said."

"Jess is right. The last thing we need is complacency. This kind of stunt requires precession timing. Hell, we don't even know if this RDX is still any good it's so old."

"I know, we're only going to get one shot at this," Devon said. "There are two ski ropes in that locker and some duct tape. Take one of the spools of wiring from Jasper's demolition box and start taping it to one of them. Make sure that the one you string the wiring on is a good twenty-five feet longer than my rope. That should give me enough distance away from the explosion."

"Okay, but I sure hope this works," Professor Stone said, opening the demolition box.

Jess stepped aboard the Whaler.

"You know," Devon said to Jess. "Yesterday, my biggest worry was losing the resort. Never thought I would be fighting to save the world from possible extinction. Hell, a lot can happen in a day."

"Don't forget about us," Jess said, embracing Devon, and giving him a kiss.

"Like I said, a lot can happen. I could get used to this."

"You better say that," Jess said.

***

The path was rutty and narrow. Sean had been fortunate so far. It had been almost ten minutes since he had left the smooth frontage road behind. He avoided the puddles whenever possible, afraid if they were too deep that the golf cart would get stuck in the mud. His body felt battered from the jarring ride over the trail.

He steered pass a grove of trees, accelerating the golf cart up another hill. The cart's motor labored while the tires spun in the mud. Reaching the summit, the cart sped down the steep hillside.

He tapped on the brake, and the pedal collapsed to the floorboard.

The golf cart careened off a boulder and tipped over, sliding on its side to the bottom of the hill.

***

Twenty minutes after leaving the boathouse, Devon signaled from the Whaler for Professor Stone to stop the Pumpkin Eater.

Professor Stone looked over his shoulder to make sure that the towline remained taut to prevent the rope from snapping when they took off again. He kept the throttle idling. Afraid that towing the dead weight of the larger Whaler had put a strain on the ski boat, the professor switched off the ignition to give the engine a rest.

He glanced at Jess, seated behind him.

"Should I hook up the wires?" Jess asked. She was holding the end of the towrope. Two exposed wires were taped to the end, ready for Jess to attach to the detonator. Fifty feet of towrope lay coiled at her feet. From there, the line reached up to the tow bar, where it was secured with a bowline knot that could be slipped off the tow bar when the time came. The remainder of the towrope extended from the ski boat's stern, out across the water to the other boat.

Another towrope was also attached to the tow bar. It, too, extended back to the Whaler, and was Devon's lifeline when he made his escape.

"We better wait and see if Devon's ready," Professor Stone said, glancing down at Jasper's shotgun on the floor for assurance.

***

Devon was freezing. He was barefoot, wearing the wetsuit he used for skiing.

The water covering the deck of the Whaler was ankle-deep and cold as ice melt. He rubbed his palms together then blew into his hands to warm them up.

He had put the tracking device on the chair behind the helm to keep it from getting wet. He watched the red blips on the green screen. The fish had chosen to position themselves apart, perhaps a survival tactic.

Devon checked the tape on the block of RDX fastened to the Fiberglas wall next to the helm. Two wires were embedded into the plastic explosive that ran along the length of towrope strung over to the Pumpkin Eater's stern. An inflated inner tube, tied to the other towrope, was lying on the bow section of the Whaler.

He got down on his knees at the hole in the Whaler's side. He picked up a ski from the deck. He lifted it over his head and slapped it hard on the water's surface. Again, he slammed the ski down, and again, repeating the motion, until he had done it ten times.

He looked over at the tracking device. One of the red blips had relocated from its original position.

It was moving toward the Whaler.

"I'll be. This klonking thing does work," he said.

Devon raised his arm and signaled the Pumpkin Eater.

Things were about to get dicey.

***

Bernie had taken a paralleling frontage road, and once they were far enough away from the accident scene, had gotten back on the freeway.

It wasn't long before he spotted an abandoned wrecker's yard and turned off.

Fenced in and missing a gate, the spot was perfect for a landing site. Victoria called Forbes and gave him their location.

After Bernie had parked the van, he and Tony got out and strolled over to irrigate some weeds. Victoria remained in the van and watched the tape one more time.

Minutes later, Bernie and Tony were catching some needed shuteye.

Bernie was sprawled up front, and Tony was taking a catnap in one of the swivel chairs with his feet up on the console. Victoria watched Tony fidget to get comfortable. She wondered how long it would take before he spilled out of the chair.

Victoria took the tape out of the player and put it on the panel next to a keyboard.

It wasn't long before she heard the helicopter making its approach.

She stared up from the van and watched the red and white Robinson R-44 with the news station's call letters stenciled on the fuselage, hover over the wrecking yard, then gradually descend.

"Wake up, you slugs, he's here," Victoria shouted.

Tony continued to doze, so Victoria slapped him on the thigh, and he jerked awake.

His foot kicked the videotape off the counter, which hit the floor and bounced out of the van, landing in a mud puddle.

Continuing to lose his balance, Tony rolled out of the chair, and was about to topple out of the van, when he caught the jam of the door and his butt came down on the running board and his feet splashed down in the puddle.

He stuck his hand in the water and came up with the smashed cassette, broken in half with the ruined tape spooling out.

"You moron!" Victoria screamed.

"Hey, don't yell at me! If you hadn't hit me, this would never have happened," Tony yelled back.

"Just grab your gear," she replied, shaking her head.

Victoria stormed out of the van, while Tony and Bernie gathered up their equipment.

The pilot set the skids of the helicopter on the ground and waved them over.

Tony and Bernie ran across the clearing, opened the door, and squeezed into the back seats. Victoria followed, occupying the seat next to the pilot.

"You know, Victoria, I'm not really authorized to be here," Miles Forbes said, handing her a headset.

"Miles, honey. We are about to make news history."

"I hope you're right. So, what time shall I be picking you up for dinner?"

"We can talk about that later. You better get us up. We can't afford to waste any more time."

"Okay. So, where to?"

"You know where Lake Recluse is?"

"I certainly do."

The chopper rose out of the abandoned wrecking yard. Once it was high enough, the craft banked to the right and headed over the rolling hills.

***

"How are you holding up?" Kate asked, putting her hand on Liz's forehead.

"To tell you the truth, not so well. My bones ache."

"That's it, we have to get you out of here."

"Rosie, sweetie, wake up," Liz said, gently shaking the dog on her lap.

"I'll carry Rosie," Kate said and picked up the dog. "Follow me."

Kate led the way to the entrance of the passage. She stole a glance toward the rear of the cave. It was too dark to see anything. She stepped from the passage and helped Liz out. They stood up and stretched.

"Come on. Jess's Bronco is just outside," Kate said, taking Liz by the hand.

They heard movement in the back of the cave.

"Run, Liz. Run!"

Kate could only go so fast, hurrying Liz along.

There was a loud rustling from behind. The silurid charged after them.

When they were finally out of the cave, Kate yelled, "Get inside the Bronco, I'll be right behind you."

The old woman scurried down the incline and ran for the Bronco.

Kate turned to distract the approaching monster, but the silurid was already outside. She stepped backward and lost her footing, dropping Rosie. They toppled down the embankment.

The silurid approached the edge and belched out a hideous grunt. The catfish's whiskers whipped about frantically like severed high-tension power lines.

Kate looked up at the towering creature. That's when something rolled out of the silurid's mouth. It was the size of a large cantaloupe, gooey, and thick with slime. The thing slid down the embankment and landed next to Kate.

She tapped her flashlight and it came on, shining on the ball-like thing.

It was a translucent globe. Inside a yellowish-brown gelatin fluid with flicks of white particles floated around an embryo.

Kate scrambled to her feet. Without weighing the consequences, she stomped on the egg sac with her boot and embryonic fluid splattered the ground.

Rosie yelped after taking one good look at the giant fish and dashed for the Bronco.

Kate could see Liz standing by the truck, not able to get inside. "Get in the Bronco!"

"Kate! The damn door is locked," Liz yelled back, tugging on the door handle.

The silurid emitted a heart-stricken sound that made Kate tremble.

"Christ, I've just killed one of its babies," Kate said, terrified and sickened by what she had done. She looked up and saw the enormous silurid push itself off the edge and slide down the embankment.

The silurid lumbered after Kate, sprinting for the Bronco.

"I'll unlock the door," she yelled, only twenty steps ahead of the monstrous fish. She ran to the driver's door and jumped inside. She flipped the switch next to the armrest, and the passenger's door lock popped up.

"Hurry, Liz! Get in!"

Liz tried to pull the door open, but the door would not budge.

"Try it again!" Kate hollered.

The silurid was only ten feet away.

Liz was pulling with all of her might, but still the door refused to open.

Kate lifted her legs up and kicked the door panel. The door unlatched and swung out.

Rosie jumped up on the passenger seat.

"Get in the back," Kate yelled at the dog. Rosie scrambled over the console onto the back seat. Liz pulled herself up into the truck and slammed the door.

Kate and Liz stared out the windshield. The fish stared back, stopping just short of the Bronco's grill.

In the headlights, the silurid was gigantic. Its body was much wider than the Bronco and could easily have been three to four times greater in length.

"It's like watching a damn horror movie at the drive-in," Liz said.

The silurid lunged upward and crashed down on the Bronco's hood, smashing the windshield.

Its mouth opened, revealing dozens of eggs crammed inside. Two eggs rolled out and oozed through the jagged edges of the shattered windshield.

"Liz, get in the back," Kate said.

Liz crawled over the console and joined Rosie.

The torn sacs ripped open and splashed on the floorboard releasing two foot-long flopping fries.

One of the hatchlings brushed up against Kate's shin.

"Ow, shit!" she yelled and jerked her foot away. "You shocked me!"

She kicked the newborn over the hump to the passenger side. The two infant catfish wiggled and floundered on the rubber mat.

Kate watched in disdain, wishing they would shrivel and die. The fish stopped flailing, moved side-by-side, and glared up at her with their milky-white eyes.

"Ah, Jesus." She turned the ignition key. The engine groaned.

The lights have gone and drained the battery!

Kate punched the switch and turned off the headlights.

She looked out the windshield and saw the silurid squirm its chest up the hood and onto the roof of the Bronco. The Fiberglas top over the cargo space began to creak. The metal portion over the cab's roof began to buckle under the immense weight of the creature.

Kate had to scrunch down so that her head wouldn't be crushed. She pumped the accelerator pedal and turned the ignition.

"Come on, start!"

The engine turned over with a rewarding roar and blue smoke belched out the twin tailpipes.

Kate slipped the transmission into reverse and stomped down on the accelerator.

The Bronco spun in the mud from the additional weight then suddenly burst free, slipping out from under the silurid, which slid down and off the hood onto the ground.

Kate shifted into drive and rammed the silurid. She reversed, stopped, and came at the fish again. More eggs spilled out of its mouth. The Bronco's all-terrain tires squashed over the eggs like they were water balloons.

"Kate!" Liz yelled, trying to warn her friend.

Kate looked down and saw the two catfish pulling themselves up over the hump with their fins. She shifted the transmission, sounded the horn, and gunned the Bronco backward. The vehicles sped back over the downed section of chain-link fence and ended up on the turnaround.

Something stabbed Kate's ankle, clear through her boot. She glanced down in pain and saw that one of the catfish had jabbed her with its barb.

"You little son of a bitch!" Kate reached across the console and opened the passenger door. She cranked the steering wheel and spun the Bronco in a tight semi-circle in the turnaround.

The newborns flew out and tumbled onto the asphalt. They quickly got their bearings and started crawling toward the lake.

"No, you don't," Kate said, stomping on the accelerator and driving over the fish.

She looked in her side mirror and saw two mashed lumps on the asphalt.

"Kate, look!" Liz said.

The silurid was down on the shore.

Kate blared the horn to scare it off.

The monstrous fish slithered into the lake.

Kate put her foot on the pedal despite the extreme pain in her ankle, and headed to the resort.

CHAPTER TWENTY-ONE

Devon laid the ski down when he heard the truck's horn. He looked over at the shore and spotted the Bronco racing toward the trailer park.

The upper rim of the sun was just peeking over the mountains. What was once consumed in the pitch of night was beginning to take shape with faint outlines. On the horizon, treetops transformed into pointy, pyramid shapes.

The gray sky became a wash of salmon-colored clouds.

Then the lake went dead calm as the wind died down. The approach of dawn brought a hush over the lake. Not even a cormorant's hoot broke the silence.

"Like the quiet before the storm," Devon muttered to himself. He looked at the screen on the tracking device.

The screen went blank.

"Damn," he said, grabbing the black box. He shook it, realizing that the battery's charge had depleted and tossed it on the deck.

"Now what?"

Suddenly, the Whaler listed to starboard. Devon lost his balance and fell onto his back. He looked up and stared directly into the face of a silurid coming up over the gunwale with its mouth stretched wide open.

Devon rolled onto his side, got to his feet, and slipped once before scampering for the bow.

***

"Start the boat!" Jess yelled, watching helplessly while the colossal silurid assaulted the Whaler.

Professor Stone turned on the ignition, and the Pumpkin Eater fired up. He gave it full throttle, and the boat roared across the water. Jess unhitched the bowline knot from the tow bar.

The towrope at Jess's feet unraveled and fed over the stern.

Jess held the detonator and watched the line, the circular pile uncoiling and became smaller and smaller. She had to time it perfectly in order for the plan to work. She looked at the Whaler; still no sign of Devon. Time was running out. Jess had to set off the charge.

She couldn't wait any longer and threw the toggle switch.

***

Devon dove onto the inner tube, yanked off the Whaler's bow seconds before Jess threw the switch. He held on for dear life and flew through the air. The inner tube hit the water, bounced, then slammed down, almost knocking the wind out of him. He fought to keep the inner tube from flipping over.

The Whaler burst apart in fiery pieces.

Devon could feel the heat on his back from the explosion. Burning chunks pelted down, sizzling the water around him.

"I don't believe it. It actually worked!" Devon yelled, waving to the figures in the Pumpkin Eater.

***

"It's Devon. Thank God," Jess yelled, slapping Professor Stone on the shoulder.

"Did we get it?"

"I think so. It happened so fast."

"We must have," he said.

Jess glanced back at what was left of the Whaler. Flames lapped up from the only remaining section of the hull. As it sank, the fire was quickly extinguished into billows of steam.

Devon was behind them, kneeling on the speeding inner tube, waving his arm like a cowpoke busting a maverick.

Jess went to wave back when she saw the silurid break the surface just behind Devon. The creature's back was burnt and charred.

The silurid torpedoed across the water, homing in for the kill.

***

Sean crawled out from beneath the golf cart. Pain stabbed up and down his left arm. He looked down and saw a red blotch on the sleeve of his parka just below the elbow. He moved his arm and heard the splintered bone scrape the lining.

He got to his feet and started down the path. He picked up his pace to a slow trot, holding his injured arm.

Less than a mile away was the steep grade that led up to the road. He had read somewhere how marathon runners could tune out the pain by focusing their minds purely on the finish line. They would be oblivious to everything around them, the competition, even the cheering fans. That was the only way they could win.

Sean focused on the road and broke into a run.

***

"Can't this thing going any faster?" Jess yelled.

"The throttle's all the way down. It's the inner tube. It's creating too much drag," Professor Stone said.

Devon was slaloming across the wake of the boat to escape the silurid.

The hellish fish sounded then burst out of the water.

Devon skipped the inner tube back across the churning water, narrowly averting the silurid plunging down.

Jess knew it was only a matter of time before Devon's luck ran out.

She saw Devon waving his arm. He was yelling something.

"I can't hear you," Jess hollered over the deafening roar of the boat's engine.

Devon yelled back, and this time, she was able to make out what he was saying.

"He wants us to whip him," Jess yelled to the professor.

"He wants us to what?"

"Devon needs to go faster. Make a hard left turn."

Professor Stone cranked the steering wheel. The boat banked to the portside, throwing Jess off balance. Her hip slammed up against the gunwale. She grabbed the lip of the Fiberglas with one hand and was able to stop from being thrown overboard.

She looked back at Devon and saw him break free from the boat's wake. He was gaining speed. The inner tube skimmed over the flat water like a hydrofoil. Devon desperately held on for the ride of his life. The inner tube was almost perpendicular to the Pumpkin Eater's starboard side.

Jess watched the silurid straining to keep up with Devon. Unable to catch its prey on the surface, the predator submerged for a surprise attack.

"We can't keep this up forever. We need to get him off the lake," Professor Stone yelled back.

"Then you better head—" but she never finished when she saw the silurid break the surface just a hundred feet in front of the boat.

How in God's name could it have traveled that fast?

And then she realized it was the other silurid.

The armored hellion charged, its ridged back displacing the water like the Nautilus in *20,000 Leagues Under the Sea* set on ramming them like Jules Verne's submarine did the clipper ship.

"Turn, turn!" Jess yelled.

"I see it," Professor Stone shouted. He tacked the boat in one direction then swung it around to avoid colliding with the silurid.

"My God, they've actually set a trap for us," Jess said.

"There's only one thing we can do," Professor Stone said.

"What's that?"

"Get rid of the inner tube."

Jess knew there was no other way and cut the rope.

CHAPTER TWENTY-TWO

Jake Walsh sat in the cab of his truck. He had parked near the landslide and was drinking coffee, listening to the radio.

He watched two of his men walk over to the bulldozers left at the base of the mudslide. The job was taking longer than he had anticipated. Every time they cleared off a section of road, the damn hill gave way and covered it up again.

"And so, after an around the clock vigilance, the levee has finally been shored up. Folks in Madison are breathing a little easier this morning. The threat of flooding has been temporarily erased from their minds, at least for now. In Washington, the scandal continues—" Jake turned off the radio.

His six-man crew was huddled together at the side of the road. What now? Jake's patience was running thin. Probably gawking at some roadkill.

He stormed out of the truck.

"Hey, what the hell's going on? This mud isn't going to clear itself."

His men ignored him.

Jake burst between two of his men to see what was so damn important.

"Donny, what's going on here?" Jake asked when he saw his foreman knelt beside a body lying in the mud.

"It's a boy. Arm's pretty busted up. Must have gotten lost in the storm," Donny said, looking up at Jake.

"Is he alive?"

"He's still breathing."

"Let's get him into my truck, and I'll run him over to Madison General."

"Hey, he moved," someone blurted.

"He's opening his eyes," Donny said.

"You got to…help us," the boy muttered.

"Don't worry, kid. You're safe now. We're going to get you to a hospital," Donny said, putting his hand on the boy's forehead.

Jake grabbed the boy under the armpits while Donny held onto the boy's legs and they carried him over to the truck.

"The catfish—" the boy mumbled.

"What did he say?" Jake asked.

"You…have to…catch them," the boy mumbled then drifted off.

"He's delirious. Must have been fishing and fell in the lake," Donny said.

"Yeah. Make sure the guys get some work done while I'm gone," Jake said.

They put the boy in the cab and buckled him up.

"Hope he's okay," Donny said, shutting the passenger door.

The kid looked terrible. Jake wasn't a religious man, but he was praying just the same for the boy to make it.

He thought to hell with the speed limit and raced down the road toward Madison.

CHAPTER TWENTY-THREE

Devon's arms felt like they were going to drop off. Every time he took a hard hit on the water, he could feel his grip slipping. He looked to his left and saw one of the silurid gaining. To his right, the other silurid was doing the same. If this continued, they would have him for sure.

He looked at Jess in the speeding boat ahead and saw her yelling at the professor behind the wheel.

The boat suddenly changed direction.

Devon shook the spray from his eyes.

That's when he realized that Professor Stone was steering directly for the shore.

The boat sped toward the beach.

Jess stood at the stern. A knife glistened in her hand.

And then he knew. It was the only way if they were to survive.

The bow of the boat was twenty feet from running up on the beach when Professor Stone banked the Pumpkin Eater, and Jess cut the towrope. The prop shot up a rooster tail as the boat headed back onto the lake.

The inner tube suddenly became unstable, impossible to control. Devon skimmed across the water at over thirty-five miles an hour straight for land. The beach was sandy, but beyond were jagged rocks and boulders with briars of stinging nettles and mesquite.

Devon tucked his head down and closed his eyes.

He tried his best to hold on when the inner tube left the water and skimmed over the beach.

The inner tube struck a rock and burst. Devon went flying. It was though he was catapulting out of a windshield during a head-on collision. He landed on his right shoulder and tumbled over some rocks, all the while executing a series of somersaults before crashing into the thistle brush.

***

Jess cried when Devon was flung into the bushes.

"Maybe now we can outrun them!" Professor Stone said.

"And then what?" Jess said.

Suddenly, a silurid surfaced just ahead of the bow.

The professor made a sharp turn. He kept his eyes glued on the great fish and gave the boat more power.

He never saw the other fish coming until it struck. Meaty chunks of burnt flesh dangled off its flank. It slammed up against the Pumpkin Eater, almost capsizing the speedboat.

And then the silurid off the bow swam up on the other side of the boat and rammed the hull. It was like being in a Volkswagen bug wedged between two transit buses barreling down the freeway.

"We can't take much more of this," Professor Stone yelled, losing control of the boat.

"Professor! Look out!" Jess yelled.

The speedboat was racing straight for the barricaded diversion tunnel.

Professor Stone and Jess ducked. The Pumpkin Eater plowed through the plywood wall and shot into the tunnel. The propeller dragged on the concrete bottom in the shallows as the water rushed in. The outboard drive ripped from the transom.

The boat continued to bash its way into the tunnel, the Fiberglas hull scraping the concaved concrete walls.

The professor braced himself behind the steering wheel.

Concrete reinforcing steel bars protruded out of the walls into the tunnel like lethal spikes constructed in a sadistic torturer's chamber. The rebar jabbed through the sides of the boat, slicing the hull.

Jess was thrown against the base of the rear seat. Jasper's box tumbled over and the contents spilled out flying everywhere. She readied herself for the inevitable. She thought of Devon; of the love they would never share; of their family they would never have.

The boat hit the concrete wall one last time and stopped.

Impaled by scores of rebar—leaning on one wall—the boat stood on its stern with the bottom of the hull facing back from where they had come. Jess held on and looked down.

A cascading waterfall spilled out of the diversion tunnel down the 100-foot chute forming a rushing river that flowed through the canyon, disappearing around a bend hidden by a stand of pine trees.

The boat teetered on the edge.

"Are you all right?" the professor asked. He was still in his seat, only staring up at the ceiling.

"I think so," Jess replied, clinging to the engine cover.

A hellish cry boomed from the other end of the diversion tunnel.

CHAPTER TWENTY-FOUR

As Devon was crawling out of the brush, he saw the Pumpkin Eater crash into the diversion tunnel. His face, hands, and legs were badly scraped up from the stinging nettles. He pulled a thorn from his cheek and one out of the palm of his right hand. Trickles of blood oozed from the numerous wounds on his body. His wetsuit was torn along his left side.

He got to his feet and ran over to the deflated inner tube. He quickly coiled up the severed towrope, picked up the inner tube, and ran over to an access ladder mounted on the cement wall of the diversion tunnel. Using one hand, he climbed up the ladder to the top.

Devon was now standing on the flat concrete expansion that was nearly the size of a football field. It would have been the flooring for the generators, pumps, and equipment that was to have controlled the dam's floodgate if the tower had been built. Rebar protruded out of the rough cement like sprouting saplings.

He sprinted over the concrete, leaving bloody footprints behind.

***

Jess peered around the gunwale of the boat and saw a silurid slithering into the tunnel—so enormous that it filled the passage—blocking out the sunlight behind it. The rebar ripped into the fish's flank as it waddled toward the boat.

"They're coming into the tunnel," Jess said.

Professor Stone slipped down from the driver's seat. He searched around and found Jasper's shotgun. He spotted something that had fallen out of Jasper's box. He picked it up. It was another block of RDX.

By now, the silurid was halfway into the tunnel.

"Here. You better have this," Stone said, handing Jess the shotgun.

She took the gun, cocked the weapon, and aimed it over the gunwale.

The silurid was almost to the boat when Jess fired a barrage of pellets, erupting a gaping wound over the creature's right eye. The gargantuan fish recoiled with pain, opened its cavernous mouth, and spewed golden spheres out onto the fast flowing water.

Jess stared in horror as they floated toward the spillway.

"Professor, it's releasing its eggs!"

"That must be Zeus. He's the mouthbreeder. He incubates the young in his mouth and guards them until they are ready to hatch. Whatever we do, we can't let them get past us!"

The professor grabbed the gaff that had been in the storage compartment and snared the first egg before it drifted by. He shook it off into the boat. The impaled embryo quivered and became still. He gaffed another then another.

"There's too many of them," Professor Stone said, swinging the gaff.

Jess fired the shotgun and splattered two egg sacs against the cement wall.

She cocked the shotgun and pulled the trigger, but nothing happened. The gun was empty.

"I'm out of shells," she yelled.

Jess turned to the professor and saw that he had a block of RDX in one hand and the detonator in his other hand. He had strung a short piece of wire between the two.

"I'm sorry, Jess. There's is no other way," he said, his hand poised on the detonator.

Suddenly, a black object appeared behind Stone.

"Professor, wait!" Jess yelled, pointing at the deflated inner tube dangling down by the ski rope outside the edge of the tunnel.

"Hey! Can you hear me down there?" a voice shouted from above.

Jess stepped around the professor, leaned out, and looked up.

Twenty feet above her head was Devon, peering down over the rim.

"Devon, thank God you're all right!"

"Grab the inner tube and I'll pull you up!"

"Do as he says," Professor Stone said.

Jess caught the inner tube, slipped it over her head, and brought it down around her waist.

"Okay, I'm ready!" she yelled up to Devon.

The silurid head-butted the hull of the Pumpkin Eater, shoving the boat so that it hung precariously close to the edge of the spillway. The black engine cover rose off the engine block, nearly taking Professor Stone with it, plummeting to the racing waters below.

Jess swung out on the rope.

"Professor, wait, we can still get you out," she pleaded.

"You know I can't do that," he replied.

"Please, don't."

"Just do me a favor. When you see Vernon, give him a message for me."

"What?" Jess said as Devon started to hoist her up.

"Tell him that a dandelion may look like a flower, but it's still just a damn weed."

Professor Stone hefted the gaff and hooked another egg sac from the water and tossed it on the boat engine's steaming manifold.

The embryo sizzled on the hot metal.

He picked up Jasper's box, held it over his head, and threw it down on another egg sack drifting near the boat.

***

Devon yanked on the rope until he was able to grab Jess's hand and pulled her up. He had anchored the towrope to a spike of rebar.

"We've got to get away from here," Jess said, stepping out of the inner tube.

"What about the professor?"

"He's going to blow the tunnel."

They took off running.

***

Professor Stone turned the toggle switch on the detonator the same moment Zeus nudged the Pumpkin Eater out over the edge of the spillway.

***

A thunderous explosion rumbled beneath Devon and Jess like an earthquake forceful enough to knock the needle clear off the Richter scale. A ball of fire burst from the diversion tunnel.

Devon could feel the heat on his back. He shielded Jess and dove on the ground. A thick cloud of smoke swept over them.

"Are you hurt?" Devon asked, sitting up to examine her.

"No, not really," she replied.

They glanced up and saw the underbelly of a helicopter hovering above them in the smoke.

"Looks like Sean got help. Good for him," Devon said, crouching with Jess while the whirlybird made its landing.

A woman and two men climbed out, one carrying a large camera on his shoulder.

"Oh, I don't believe it. News reporters?" Devon said with disgust.

"Devon, we can't tell them about this."

"You're right. Not till we sort this all out. You stall them. I'm going to check the spillway," Devon said.

"The professor couldn't have possibly survived the blast."

"I know, but I still have to look."

"Go. I'll hold them off," Jess said.

They converged on her like a feverish pack of hounds cornering a defenseless fox.

The news reporter shoved the microphone in Jess's face as she stood.

"Do you mind?" Jess said and pushed the microphone away.

"Hold on, Victoria. I'm not ready," said the man carrying the recorder attached by a cord to the microphone in Victoria's hand.

"Hurry up, Bernie. We don't have all day," Victoria snapped. "Name."

"What?" Jess asked.

"What is your name?"

"Jess Murdock." Jess wanted to slap the rude woman.

"Murdock. By any chance, are you related to a Vernon Murdock?" Victoria asked.

"He's my brother. Why?" Jess wondered how she could possibly know Vernon. She glanced over at Devon standing by the concrete rubble next to a wide fissure caused by the blast. He was leaning forward with his hands on his knees, peering over the edge.

"We know about his experiment," Victoria said.

"What on earth are you talking about?"

"We've seen the tape."

"Tape! What tape?"

"Tony found it at the hatchery. It has your brother and—"

"For Christ's sake, Victoria, shut up!" Tony protested.

"And where's this tape?" Jess asked. She could not believe it. They had pilfered the Quonset hut. Taken the tape without her permission. But weren't the tapes all ruined?

Of course, the VCR, they had forgotten to check the VCR.

"You needn't get excited," Tony said to Jess. "The tape was destroyed."

"I can't believe you people."

"Tell Miles to go up and see where that smoke is coming from," Victoria yelled at Bernie.

Jess watched the audio technician set down his equipment and run over to the helicopter.

She glanced back to the spot where Devon was standing.

He was gone.

CHAPTER TWENTY-FIVE

When no one was looking, Devon threw the inner tube over the edge and shimmied down the rope. The view below looked like the aftermath of a bomber raid with fiery clumps of what was left of the Pumpkin Eater and the silurid strewn over the rocks, most of which had washed downstream.

He stepped one foot onto the inner tube and swung himself into the tunnel. He grabbed onto a bent shank of rebar and began pulling himself along the wall before letting go of the inner tube. The inner tube swayed back and forth, dangling just within reach. He held his free hand over his mouth so he could breathe without inhaling the smoke.

The rushing water was up to his waist. There were fragments of his boat and fleshy smears blasted into the concrete. The explosion had jaggedly routed out the diversion tunnel by more than twenty feet. Mist and smoke prevented him from seeing more than ten feet ahead.

Suddenly, Devon heard a crackling sound creep through the tunnel—and then a strange tingling sensation in his legs. He turned his head.

Athena emerged out of the smoke. The silurid's head and sides had been ravaged from the Whaler explosion. Ragged bits of torn flesh dangled from its gouged skin.

Devon turned and dove for the inner tube. The silurid lunged after him.

He grabbed the lifeline and swung out away from the mouth of the tunnel. He clawed at the concrete wall, digging his fingertips into a cement niche.

Wind buffeted his back. He turned and saw the chopper coming down. Devon could see the pilot through the glass, one hand on the joystick.

The thirty-foot silurid lunged out of the tunnel, almost gracefully, before landing on the helicopter's gyrating blades.

Devon caught a fleeting glimpse of the fearful look on the pilot's face.

The sharp rotors shred Athena's head, then broke off the mast, forcing the chopper's tail boom to tilt earthward.

The decapitated silurid and disabled helicopter plunged onto the boulders below, rupturing the fuel tank, and sending everything flying in a rising ball of fire.

***

Tony and Bernie ran after Jess. She rushed over to the edge of the spillway.

Both men grabbed the ski rope and hauled Devon up. He climbed onto the cement and sat down on the edge. Down below, the burning wreckage was quickly being disassembled by the discharging spillway, and swept downriver.

Jess sat down next to Devon.

"You had me worried," she said.

"I know. I'm sorry."

"What happened?" Bernie asked.

"Your pilot got too close to the spillway," Devon said.

"We're screwed blue, now," Tony said.

"Yeah, looks like we better start updating our resumes," Bernie said.

"Not so fast," Victoria said, strolling over. "Don't forget there's a story here. And I want it!" Victoria Savage bellowed.

"There's no story here, you callous bitch," Jess said.

"Hey, you watch who you're calling a bitch."

"Doesn't it even bother you that your pilot is dead? After you told him to fly down there."

"He shouldn't have gotten so close."

"You're really something," Jess said.

"Hey, you guys wouldn't by chance have a cell phone, would you?" Devon asked.

"No, but she does," Tony said, and snatched the phone out of Victoria's coat pocket. He handed it over to Devon.

"Hey, that's mine."

"Don't you ever know when to quit? You know, Bernie and I aren't going to take the heat for you on this one. The general manager isn't going to think too kindly of you when he finds out how you tricked Forbes into coming here. You know what? I think your career just took a major dump. What do you think, Bernie?"

"A *major* dump!" Bernie unplugged the microphone cord from his recorder.

Jess heard something fall on the cement.

She looked down and saw that Victoria had dropped her microphone.

Jess nudged it over the edge of the spillway with her boot.

CHAPTER TWENTY-SIX

Five days later, Peter Sykes and his girlfriend, Cindy Briggs, were night fishing in San Francisco Bay. It was a great night for angling. The tide was up, the wind was down, and he could not have wanted for better company. He shoved the ten-foot-long surf rod into the pole holder.

Following the beam of his flashlight, he gingerly stepped across the slippery boulders and made his way up to the truck.

Cindy sat on the tailgate, bundled up in a blanket.

Peter ran over and hopped up beside her. The springs on the truck squeaked in protest.

"When you asked me if I liked fish, I thought you were taking me out for a nice dinner. This isn't quite what I had in mind," Cindy said.

"Anyone can go to a restaurant and eat fish. It's not everyone that can actually catch them. Trust me, this will be fun. Here, have some coffee. This will warm you up. It's my special blend." Peter took a thermos and poured some of the contents into a cup. He handed the cup to Cindy.

"Careful it's—"

"Jesus," she said, having already taken a sip.

"Hot," he finished.

"Strong, you mean! What the heck is in here?"

"Some Kahlua, a little rum."

"Maybe some coffee?" She took another sip anyway.

"You don't like it?"

"I guess it's not bad," Cindy said, and smiled.

"Now, look around. What restaurant has a view like this? There's the city, Alcatraz, Marin, you can even see the bridge,"

Peter said, pointing out San Francisco, the defunct prison site, the town across the bay, and the Golden Gate Bridge.

"This is sort of nice," Cindy purred, taking another drink.

"Call me a romantic," Peter said.

"All right." Cindy leaned over and gave Peter a kiss.

Peter put his arm around Cindy's shoulder.

"What's that?" she said, breaking off the kiss.

"What's what?"

"In the water."

Peter turned and saw something floating in the bay, radiating from the yellowish glow of the lamppost near his truck. "I don't know."

"Go see," Cindy said.

"Okay," he said reluctantly.

He scooted down off the tailgate. When his feet hit the asphalt, he realized that his special blend had made him a little wobbly on his feet.

He took his time, not wanting to embarrass himself by slipping on the algae-covered rocks and directed his flashlight out on the water.

There was something out there all right, but it was difficult to see in the dark. He crept out as far as he could without falling in.

The two objects floated closer. They were globular, the size of soccer balls.

"Peter! Look!"

"What's wrong?" he asked, startled as he turned around.

"Your pole! I think you have a fish," Cindy said.

Peter scurried back over the rocks and reached for his fishing rod. He picked up the rig and gave it a quick jerk to set the hook and cranked the handle on the reel.

Whatever it was, it was big.

After a few minutes of angling, Peter yanked the catch from the water.

"What is it?" Cindy called down.

Peter bent over, stuck his forefinger into the gill of the fish, and held it up.

"It's a halibut. Good size one. Maybe three pounds." He stuck his pole back into the holder and pulled them both up then walked back to the truck with the fish.

"Good. Now we can eat," Cindy said.

"Sure. Let's go to my place and I'll fix it up."

"Yeah, you better be doing the cooking. I'm not touching that thing until it's on my plate," Cindy said, scooting off the tailgate.

Peter threw the fish into a bucket and laid his pole in the bed. He folded up the tailgate, and joined Cindy in the cab.

He started up the truck.

"What were those things out in the water?" Cindy asked while Peter drove.

"I'm not exactly sure, probably those glass balls the Japanese fishermen use to float over their crab pots, so they can find them later. They must have drifted in from sea. You'd be surprised what ends up in the bay," he replied.

Peter shifted into second and drove onto the freeway entrance.

**

Out in the bay, the orbs floated in the notoriously strong current that flowed out beneath the Golden Gate Bridge. Beyond was the Pacific Ocean with its vast aquamarine ecosystem.

The ocean waves beckoned.

CHAPTER TWENTY-SEVEN

Lake Recluse—10 Months Later

Kelly leaned out the booth and waved off the truck with a bass boat hitched to its rear bumper.

"Sorry, folks. We're all booked up," she hollered and hung up the *Campgrounds are Full* sign outside the main gate.

Before locking up, she checked her French braid in the mirror. She loved the way the brunette strands intertwined with the blond ones.

She went outside, climbed into a golf cart, and headed down the road to the country store. She could not believe how many people had showed up for the bass derby.

Local anglers, fishermen from all over the county, even those from out of state had come in droves for the first annual event.

Lake Recluse was once again a sport fishing paradise, thanks to the insatiable silurids that had eradicated the destructive population of bottom-feeding carp.

Kelly detoured down a lane winding through the trailer park. Every mobile home was occupied for the summer. She drove by the endless rows of boat trailers hitched to vehicles in the marina parking lot.

A young couple walking their dog gave her a friendly wave.

"Morning," Kelly replied with a cheery grin.

She pulled off onto the shoulder to make room for a Murdock Fish Hatchery tanker and a Madison Beverage Company delivery truck to pass by. She had a great view of the bustling campgrounds. Campers huddled around picnic tables preparing breakfast on camp stoves and barbeque pits. Late risers crawled out of pup and dome tents for their first breath of crisp, mountain air.

Kelly went down the hill and parked the golf cart next to the store. She got out and went inside. The place was packed. She squeezed by busy shoppers to the back of the counter where Kate and Devon were busy ringing up customers, issuing fishing licenses, and explaining the rules of the Joyner & Talbert Fish Derby honorably named in memoriam after their dear friends, Jasper and Claude.

***

Devon stepped out of the trailer carrying a frosted cake with lit candles.

Sean, Nell, and Liz sat on one side of the table, Jess and Kelly on the other.

"Happy birthday!" everyone sang out.

"That looks lovely," Kate said from the head of the table.

"Make a wish, Mom," Nell said.

"That's going to be hard," Kate replied.

"Why, Mom?"

Kate glanced about the table. "I have everything right here. What more could I ask for?"

"Then pretend, okay. I want some cake," Nell said, making everyone laugh.

"Okay." Kate rolled her eyes, took a deep breath, and blew out all the candles.

"I want a big piece," Nell said.

"Mom, I better make the rounds before it gets too late," Sean said, standing up from the table.

"Take some cake with you then," Kate said, cutting him a slice to put on a napkin.

"Thanks, Mom." Sean took the offering and started across the patio.

"Can I go, too?" Nell asked.

"Yes, you may. But stay out of trouble. I'm warning you," Kate said.

Max trotted over and laid his head on Nell's lap.

"Not now, Max," Nell said. She folded her cake in a napkin then ran off to catch up with Sean.

Rejected, Max wandered back to the bassinet where Rosie was nursing her litter of pups. He flopped down in a huff. He leaned his head over and gave one of the pups a raspy lick.

"He's such the proud father," Liz said, taking a bite of cake.

"And she's such the good mother," Kate replied.

***

Late into the evening darkness crept over Lake Recluse.

Sitting in lawn chairs on the porch, Devon and Jess gazed out on the moonlit lake.

Campfires flickered about the resort like dancing lightning bugs.

Though it was a mild evening, Jess had a blanket up around her shoulders.

Her cellular phone was on the table next to her chair. She rarely ventured far without it.

"Kyle called," Jess said.

"Oh yeah, how's he doing?"

"He got accepted at Woods Hole Oceanographic Institute."

"Good for him," Devon said.

"Oh, and Vernon called."

"So, what's that lunatic brother of yours up to these days?"

"Devon! That's terrible."

"I'm just kidding. What did he have to say?"

"Only that they've been keeping him pretty busy."

"Good. That'll keep him out of trouble. I wonder how Billy and Gus are managing with us gone."

"They're probably glad to be rid of us for a few days," Jess said. Since the wedding last year, she and Devon were spending more time at the lake and less time operating the fish hatchery.

"Yeah, I guess I can be a pain in the ass at times," Devon said.

"Oh, you have your moments of grandeur."

Jess looked over her shoulder and saw Kate coming out to join them. She walked over with a slight limp, pulled up a lawn chair, and sat down next to Jess.

Kate put her cellular phone down on the table next to Jess's.

"Such a beautiful night," Kate said, bending to massage her ankle.

"Yeah, it doesn't get any better than this," Devon said.

"Oh, but it does. Jess, may I?" Kate asked.

"Of course," Jess said and opened the blanket. Kate held out her hands while Jess gave her baby to her mother-in-law. Jess passed Kate the blanket.

"Now, my day is complete. And how is our little Jonathan tonight?" Kate said, bundling the baby up in the blanket.

Still asleep, Jonathan smiled and cooed at her voice.

The moon's reflection graced the calm lake under an ebony dome sprinkled with a million stars. Only the distant hoot of a cormorant broke the stillness of the night.

Jess could feel Devon's arm on her shoulder. She rested up against her husband.

Kate rocked baby Jonathan.

The family sat silently, enjoying each other's company and reveled in the serenity of Lake Recluse.

CHAPTER TWENTY-EIGHT

The fog crept into the bay on schedule shrouding the Golden Gate Bridge, leaving only the orange peaks with their warning beacons visible.

She took one last look at the piers jutting out of Fisherman's Wharf and stepped inside the Telegraph Hill coffee shop.

Her name was Vanessa. Vanessa Simmons.

She had picked website designer for her occupation. She jogged every other day and loved eco-thrillers. She had been an activist for an environmental group, though she had not yet decided which one, but could throw a name out there fast if he should ask. She would be candid if need be, but not overly opinionated so as not to scare him off.

The establishment was crowded. She went up to the counter and ordered a latte with a Danish. The young man behind the counter quickly grabbed a tray. He whipped up the frothy beverage, placed the pastry on a small plate, and rang up the sale. She pulled her money from her purse.

"Thanks," she said, slipping the strap of her purse over her shoulder and picking up the tray. She pretended to glance indecisively about the dining area then ambled over to the small table set against one of the windows, eyeing the unoccupied chair across from the man busily writing in a notebook.

"Is this seat taken?" she asked.

"No, but I'd rather…"

She let the purse strap slip off her shoulder and clumsily leveled her tray in the nick of time to avoid spilling her latte.

The man flinched and looked around the congested coffee shop.

"I'm sorry. I didn't realize it was this crowded. Please, sit down."

"Thanks," she said and set her tray on the table. She removed her purse from her shoulder and placed it next to the sugar dispenser. She left the flap slightly open, but not enough so that he could see inside.

"That was rude of me," he said. His face had flushed with embarrassment.

"We all value our own space. I hope I'm not intruding."

"Not at all."

"Are you a writer?" she asked, breaking off a morsel of Danish and slipping it into her mouth.

"Ah, no, not exactly. I'm a biologist."

"That must be interesting work. What field?"

"Marine," he said. He closed his book, put his pen down, and took a sip of his coffee.

"A marine biologist. How strange."

"What's strange?" he asked.

"I just spent the day at the Steinhart Aquarium with a girlfriend of mine. Funny bumping into you, you a marine biologist and all."

"How was it? The aquarium. Did you enjoy yourself? You and your girlfriend?"

"I found it fascinating." She had a friend's name on the tip of her tongue, just in case he should ask.

"You did?" His face relaxed into a smile.

"So, where do you work when you're a marine biologist?"

"The Scripps Institution of Oceanography. It's a research facility in La Jolla. They stationed me up here to conduct some studies. Ever hear of it?"

"Yes, I have. Have you been with them long?"

"Not long," he said.

"So what are you working on?"

"Has to do with the maximum sustainable yield."

"I'm sorry, the what?"

"It's the maximum amount of fish that can be caught each year without impairing the population growth. In the past six months, fishermen have reported an alarming decrease in the population levels off the Pacific Coast."

"Oh my. And what would cause that?"

He was about to reply when he stopped himself. He studied her for a moment.

"I'm sorry," she said with a shrug. "There I go again. Bad habit of mine, asking too many questions. I guess I'm just a little nervous." She glanced away and saw a couple vacating a table. "I'm sorry for bothering you," she said and began to pick up her tray.

"No, no. It's all right. Don't be silly. Please. Stay," he said, placing his hand on her wrist.

"Only if you insist."

"I insist."

"Maybe I should introduce myself. I'm Vanessa Simmons." She held out her hand.

"Vernon Murdock," he said and shook her hand. He was not in a great hurry to release the grip. She liked that; it was working.

Once he pulled his hand away, she lifted up her cup with both hands and peered at him through the steam. He sat back in his chair, watching her. The corners of his mouth swept up into a sly grin.

"What?" she asked.

"I spend so much time with my work, I almost forgot how nice it is to just relax and talk."

"You should do it more often. It seems to agree with you," she told him.

He glanced down at his watch. "Oh my, I didn't realize the time. I should go. Perhaps I could see you again?" he asked, stuffing his binder into a backpack.

"I'd like that. Let me give you my number. I better get yours, too, just in case you have trouble reaching me." She wrote down her phone number and got his.

"Then I'll see you later, Vanessa?"

"I'm counting on it," she said. She watched him leave the coffee shop and waited until he was far enough down the street before picking up her purse and putting it on her lap.

She pretended to rummage through her handbag and switched off the tape recorder. She took out her cellular phone and punched in the numbers before putting the phone to her ear.

"Hello, Mrs. Constantino? This is Victoria Savage. Yes, I do believe I will be subletting the apartment after all. Yes, a six-month lease would be fine. I'll bring the deposit over tomorrow. Yes, you too. Bye now."

She put the cellular phone back in her purse. She sipped her latte, staring out the window, and pondered like a Grand Master at a chess tournament, contemplating her next move.

PART TWO

THE SILURID DOMAIN

CHAPTER TWENTY-NINE

Galapagos Islands—San Cristobal Island

Steve McKay, marine biologist and tour guide at the Charles Darwin Research Center sat on a grassy knoll with the four tourists in his group. They were enjoying their lunch while a hundred yards away heavy waves pounded the rocky shore.

"When Charles Darwin first came here in eighteen thirty-five, there were an estimated two-hundred and fifty thousand giant tortoises populating the Galapagos Islands. Now, there are only fifteen hundred," Steve said.

Dora and Mike Westlake shook their heads in disbelief. Retirees, they had been traveling the world, soaking up new lifetime experiences, and squandering their children's inheritance.

"How tragic," Dora commented.

"I'll say," Mike said. "So what caused them to die off?"

"Well, the tortoises had no reason to fear man. Commercial hunters and whalers contributed to most of the declining tortoise population."

"Such senseless slaughter. Kind of like the American buffalo," Mike said.

"Bison, dear," Dora said, correcting her husband.

"What? Bison, buffalo, same thing."

Steve paused to take a bite out of his sandwich and smiled at the other couple.

Philip and Lorrie Riker were newlyweds, Green Peace activists and environmentalists, visiting the Galapagos Islands for their honeymoon. They waited tentatively while Steve swallowed. He continued by saying, "Hmm, not exactly, Mike. Don't take me wrong. I by no means condone what they did, but times were harsh back in those days. Ships didn't have refrigeration, so it was difficult to preserve food supplies. Sailors suffered from malnutrition, scurvy, rickets, you name it."

"But once the tortoises were killed, wouldn't the meat spoil?" Lorrie asked.

"They could have cured the meat by smoking it," Philip said. "Just like beef jerky. Right, Steve?"

"Well, Philip, I wish that was the case. You see a tortoise can live up to fourteen months without food or water."

"You can't be serious," Mike said.

"Oh, I am. The sailors would capture the tortoises alive. Then they'd stack them in the hold of the ship, one on top of the other on their backs. Tortoises were often referred to as *Galapagos mutton.*"

"That's just damn right cruel," Lorrie said, putting her hand up to her mouth as if she might throw up her lunch.

"Fortunately, in nineteen fifty-nine, the Galapagos Islands were declared a national park, and now the giant tortoises are protected," Steve said.

Mike removed his hat and combed his thinning hair with his fingers.

"So, I gather Darwin wasn't here to save the tortoises from extinction," he said.

"It was too early for that. He came here primarily to study them and formulated his concept of evolution through natural selection."

"Natural selection?" Dora asked.

"It's a term referring to when certain species become dominant over other species; even to the extent of reducing their numbers or even driving the subordinate animals into extinction," Steve said.

"Survival of the fittest," Mike piped in.

"Exactly," Steve responded and also added, "The giant tortoises are a prime example. Darwin discovered that depending on the terrain that they had to adapt to, the tortoises on each island became separate species, even subspecies. Of course, it also helps to be able to live to be one-hundred and fifty years old."

"No wonder they move so slow," Dora chuckled.

"So, everyone up for a little hike?" Steve asked. "I promise it won't be too strenuous. There are four-hundred and fifty land tortoises here on San Cristobal Island, so I'm sure we'll be able to spot a few. I'm hoping to see sea turtles at the beach."

The group gathered up the blankets and lunch bags and proceeded single file behind Steve down the well-traveled dirt path.

Frigate birds soared high in the azure, gliding the wind currents in a cyclone pattern.

Steve pointed out a giant iguana, scurrying between two rocks. A few minutes later, they paused to watch ten 300-pound giant tortoises graze, their thick necks stretched out of their protective shells, beak mouths nibbling on thorny thickets.

White cap combers crashed on the boulders bordering a cove.

"Where is that God-awful smell coming from?" Lorrie asked, stepping off a rock onto the beach.

"I don't know, but it sure is foul," Philip said, holding his nose.

Steve strode around a boulder and stopped. The others warily came up behind him.

Three decomposing seals and hundreds of dead fish littered the beach with even more limp bodies floating ashore on the incoming surf.

"Oh, Mike, I think I'm going to be sick," Dora said. Mike put his arm around his wife to steady her.

"Come on," he said and led her away.

"Steve, what's that over there?" Philip asked.

Steve, Philip, and Lorrie walked across the sand and approached two sea turtles seemingly washed ashore.

"Oh no! Not them, too!" Steve blurted.

"What is it?" Lorrie asked.

"It's Gorge and Maria."

"They actually have names?" Philip asked.

"Yes. Those black boxes attached to their backs are GPS tracking devices."

"That seems a little cruel," Lorrie said.

"Not at all. They're light enough. Besides, after a period of time, once the transmitters quit, they eventually drop off. This is really devastating. We were hoping to map Gorge and Maria's mating habits by tracking them via satellite. We even set up an Internet Web site so that if people spotted the sea turtles, they could report when and where they saw them."

Lorrie knelt in the sand to get a closer look at one of the sea turtles, its lifeless head extended out the shell. She stroked the dead creature's head. The stenciled name *Maria* and a series of numbers were painted on the shell.

She glanced over at the other sea turtle—its identifier *Gorge*—and was shocked to see that the determined aquatic reptile was still alive and was dragging itself across the sand by its front flippers to be near Maria.

"Thank God," Steve said.

"Sorry, Gorge," Lorrie said, tearing up. "I'm afraid she's dead."

Gorge nudged his head against Maria's head in an attempt to revive his companion.

Mike trudged through the sand and joined them.

"Dora will be fine in a bit." He surveyed the dead fish. "What in the world could have done this?"

"I'm not completely sure," Steve said. He went over and knelt to examine some of the fish. "Strangest thing I've ever seen. There are no defensive wounds, no visible wounds at all and no sign of toxin rejection."

"Looks almost as if they were struck by lightning," Mike said.

"We haven't had a storm in months," Steve said.

"Hey, you guys! Look!" Lorrie called out as Philip pointed.

Steve and Mike turned and saw Gorge paddling into the water. The sea turtle quickly met an incoming wave and submerged under the breaking foam.

"Where do you think he's off to?" Mike asked.

"I have no idea," was all Steve could say. He stared bewildered and watched Gorge swim out into the ocean.

CHAPTER THIRTY

Bolsa Chica State Beach—Southern California—Three Months Later

Arty Nelson and Leo Carr carried their lit lanterns and buckets across a patch of lawn overlooking the beach. They wore sweatshirts and shorts, as the night was balmy, only Arty had on sneakers where Leo wore flip-flops.

Small waves unfurled and rolled ashore, sparkling like tumbling gems under the full moon.

"Where is everyone? I thought you said this was a big deal," Arty said.

"It is. We're just early, that's all," Leo replied.

"Are you sure they're in season?"

"Of course."

Arty suddenly stopped when they reached the picnic tables by the state park's public restrooms. "Ah, geez, I gotta go!"

"Can't you wait?"

"No. I gotta go," Arty said and set his bucket on a picnic bench.

"Told you not to eat those chili dogs."

"What, and pass up the buy one, get one free senior discount? Not in your life, buddy boy. Hey, won't kill you to wait." Arty held up his lantern and headed for the men's side of the restroom.

"Sorry, pal!" Leo said. "Kind of ironic, wouldn't you say? I get you to go on your first grunion run and you get the runs?" Leo laughed. "Hurry it up. I'll be down by the water filling my bucket."

"Fine, fine," Arty said and scurried into the public restroom. He could hear the fading flapping of Leo's flip-flops as his friend headed out onto the sand.

Arty raised his lantern and peered inside the restroom. There were some crumpled paper towels on the concrete floor next to the refuse can. He rushed by the sinks and bolted into the first stall.

He placed the lantern on the floor by his feet, pulled down his shorts and squatted on the toilet seat just in the nick of time.

When Leo reached the water's edge thousands of tiny grunion were already scampering out of the surf onto the wet sand to spawn. He put down his lantern and chased after the fingerlings with his bucket. His flip-flops flapped even louder when he scurried across the hard-packed sand, scooping up grunion by the handfuls and tossing them into the pail.

Back in the restroom, Arty was finishing purging himself with one last explosive gush. "Oh, never again," he swore and reached for the toilet roll. He pulled down and got only a couple squares before the paper pulled off the cardboard tube. "Swell, just swell."

A loud crash outside his stall made him jump.

"Leo? Is that you?"

Something banged against the metal refuse can.

"Leo! Quit screwing around!"

Arty pulled up his pants, picked up his lantern, and opened the stall door.

The glowing light shone about the restroom, but there was no one there.

Arty figured to hell with washing his hands and went directly for the exit.

He was just passing the refuse can when something lurched up and clambered across his back.

"Holy shit!" Arty yelled at the raccoon, racing across the floor and dashing outside.

On the beach, Leo already had a full bucket of squirming grunion and was walking back to his lantern.

Suddenly, the casting light was blocked by a dark, looming shadow that stretched across the sand.

Leo looked up and instantly there was terror in his eyes. He fell back on the sand and began scrambling back on his hands and feet like a fleeing crab.

Arty came out of the restroom and grabbed his bucket off the picnic bench. He followed Leo's footprints in the sand until he reached Leo's lantern.

Leo's bucket was knocked over. Most of the captured grunion had already escaped and were wriggling back into the water.

There was no sign of Leo.

"Leo?" Arty called out.

He looked down and saw a set of footprints. He followed them for a short distance and soon found Leo's flip-flops left in the sand next to a deep furrowed impression that had to be more than ten feet wide leading into the water.

Arty stood in a daze.

The frothy surf washed ashore, claimed Leo's flip-flops and swept them out into the ocean.

CHAPTER THIRTY-ONE

Los Angeles International Airport

The underbelly of the 747 made its approach, low enough to peel the paint off the rooftops of the morning commute traffic. The jumbo jet cleared the sound barrier and touched down, tires screeching and smoking on the tarmac.

Twenty minutes later, Devon and Jess were lugging their travel bags down the busy corridor through the LAX terminal. They were passing by a bank of telephones when Jess stopped.

"Shouldn't we call Kate? Let her know we got in okay."

"Tell it like it is. You just want to know how Jonathan's doing."

"It is our first time away from him."

"And this is our honeymoon. True, it's a couple years overdue."

"I'm just excited as you are to get to Catalina, but couldn't we just call?"

"All right." Devon smiled. He put the suitcases down by the wall.

He picked up a telephone receiver and dialed collect.

"Hello, Mom? We made it. No, we're still at the airport. Not bad. Jess was...I mean we were wondering how Jonathan was doing?"

At the resort, Kate was standing in her kitchen keeping an eye on fourteen-month-old Jonathan, crawling across the floor. He paused, fascinated by the dog dish and stared into the bowl.

Max sat a couple feet away, observing the boy with close interest.

Jonathan reached into the bowl and grabbed a small handful of dried nuggets.

The golden retriever perked up his ears.

"Jonathan? Oh, he's having breakfast." She cupped her hand over the phone and said in a stern whisper, "Jonathan! Get away from there! Leave Max's food alone!"

Jonathan peered up at Kate and munched on a nugget. He grinned, brown drool running down his chin.

Kate took her hand off the phone.

"Tell Jess not to worry. Jonathan's fine. Just enjoy yourselves. Oh, by the way, the reservations are all set for the delta. Now, you two go and have fun. We'll see you in a couple of days. Love you. Bye."

Kate hung up the phone just in time to see Jonathan giggling and Max licking the boy's face.

"You two."

CHAPTER THIRTY-TWO

Playa Del Rey State Beach—Southern California

Hundreds of umbrellas and many more sunbathers were sprawled on their beach towels, baking under the torrid sun.

There were sun-worshipers playing volleyball and crowds of people in the surf. A concession stand was set up with a long line of bronze teenagers, girls in thong bikinis and boys in hotdog surfer shorts waiting to place their orders.

A barefoot man in a Hawaiian shirt and denim cutoffs hurried across the hot sand carrying a large cooler and an umbrella. He stopped and danced in place to cool off his burning feet then continued on for a few more steps only to repeat the ritual.

Lifeguards towers were lined along the waterfront, each man and woman poised for action, scanning the shallow waters for swimmers in trouble or the potential threat of a shark attack. The six-foot waves were breaking in steady sets perfect for body surfing and boogie boarding.

A teenage boy on a lime-green boogie board rode the crest of a wave and skimmed in on the foam. He quickly stood up, turned the nose of his board around, dove back on, and paddled back into the surf.

Brooke, and her sister, Amber, were lying side by side on their beach towels, staring out at the water. Their friend, Tiffany, was next to Brooke, and had fallen asleep with her bikini top unsnapped so that she could get an even tan on her fair skin. Brooke had just finished arranging pennies on Tiffany's bare back.

"She's going to kill you," Amber whispered.

Instead of answering, Brooke motioned for her sister to check out a guy parading down the beach. The absurdly muscular bodybuilder in his tight-fitting Speedo swim trunks sensed the girls staring and flexed.

"That's what I call hunkalicious," Brooke said.

"I think he's already taken," Amber said.

"By who?"

"By himself."

A lean surfer with long sandy-blond hair darted by.

"Now, don't tell me he's not cute," Brooke said.

"Eh. He's okay."

"Oh, right, I forgot. He's no Vinnie Vedderman. I can't believe you're still dating that creep after last weekend."

"How was I to know the stud in his tongue was going to get hooked on my braces?"

"You're lucky I showed up and found the pliers before Dad got home," Brooke said.

"You're just jealous I have a boyfriend."

"Yeah, like I'd want Vinnie Vedderman's fat icky tongue flopping around in my mouth for two hours."

They craned their necks as a young man walked in front of them. He had straggly shoulder-length black hair and a thick fu Manchu and was inappropriately dressed for the sweltering heat in a black leather jacket, black jeans, and black motorcycle boots. He ignored the girls and strode by.

"Now, he's cool," said Amber.

"Hey, get a load of Ben," Brooke said.

Ben shot down a wave and rode it out onto the sand. He picked up his boogie board and ran over to his sisters.

He stuck the nose of his board into the sand and shook his wet hair, sprinkling Tiffany on the back, causing her to wake in a start.

"Hey! Watch it!"

"You've got to go in. The water's great," Ben said. He snatched Tiffany's soda and finished it off in one gulp then crumbled the aluminum can and tossed it back on Tiffany's beach towel.

"Jerk-off!"

Ben spun around, grabbed his boogie board, and headed back out into the water.

"I'm getting hot. Let's go in," Amber said.

Amber and Brooke stood and adjusted their bikinis.

Tiffany reached back to snap her top. She went to get up and felt the pennies slide off her back.

"What the—"

Fifty yards away, a lifeguard standing on the deck of his tower spotted something with his binoculars. A twenty-foot long dark shape was beneath the surface out where the waves were forming. He quickly dropped the binoculars lanyard around his neck and grabbed his walkie-talkie.

"This is tower five. I have a possible shark alert."

"Are you sure it's not a bed of kelp?" a woman asked.

"Maybe, but we better not chance it."

"Stations respond. Get everyone out of the water!"

The lifeguard jumped from the tower onto the sand and raced toward the water.

A hundred feet out, a body surfer jumped up to see farther out. A giant swell was beginning to form into what could be a ten-foot wave.

"Outside! Outside!" he yelled to the others.

Twenty other bodysurfers set up for the wave. Ben was among them. He turned the nose of his boogie board around. The wave began to take shape, rolling up into a white-crested peak. The bodysurfers poured it on, swimming as fast as they could.

Ben paddled with everything he had.

The wave curled with only the bodysurfers' heads and shoulders protruding out of the surf.

A great white shark thrust its head out of the wave between two bodysurfers, its mouth gaping wide enough to swallow a man whole.

Ben looked over his shoulder and saw the shark directly behind him.

"Oh my God!" he screamed and paddled for his life.

Amber, Brooke, and Tiffany were splashing each other when Brooke stopped to look at the approaching wave.

The wave broke, and the shark came down on Ben.

"Ben!" She watched her brother swept under.

A white jeep wagon drove up on the sand. Three lifeguards jumped out and ran over, motioning for swimmers to get out of the water, which created mayhem as people scrambled, stumbling and falling to get to safety.

Ben's lime-green boogie board washed ashore—and then everyone backed away.

The enormous great white slid up on the beach with its mouth agape, bearing its razor sharp teeth.

Brooke screamed and ran over to one of the lifeguards.

"Somebody do something! It's eaten my brother! Please help him!"

Tiffany and Amber held onto Brooke's arm, afraid that she would get too close to the deadly predator.

A lifeguard warily approached the shark and kicked it. The shark did not move.

"It's dead."

"Get me out of here," came a muffled voice.

The lifeguard knelt and looked inside the shark's enormous mouth and peered down its gullet.

"I see him. I don't believe it. Somebody go grab some towels so we can flip this thing over."

Four lifeguards and six other men used towels to protect their hands from the shark's rough skin. They turned the shark over on its side, exposing a craterous gash in its belly. Ropy entrails slopped out of the cavity like cooked spaghetti sliding out of a pot.

Ben was entangled in the shark's intestines. The smell was nauseating.

"Come on, I'm dying in here," Ben pleaded.

The lifeguards pulled Ben out.

"Ben, thank God you're alive!" Brooke shouted.

Ben staggered to his feet, wiping the offensive gore off his face and chest. He looked down at the gutted shark.

"What tore into him?" Ben wondered aloud.

"I don't know," said the lifeguard, "but whatever it was, it was more than a match for a great white."

CHAPTER THIRTY-THREE

Catalina Island—Southern California

After the Starship Express ferry had tied up in Avalon Bay, Devon and Jess disembarked and carried their bags down the wharf a short distance to the Catalina Island Inn where they checked in and went up to their room.

They dropped their bags at the foot of the queen-size bed not bothering to unpack and stepped out on the veranda overlooking the Avalon Bay Marina and the Catalina Casino.

"Some view," Devon said.

"It's beautiful," Jess said, holding onto the railing.

"So, what do you want to do? We could go hiking or rent jet skis, your call. If you want, we could go visit the Wrigley Mansion."

"You mean like the chewing gum?"

"Yep. It said in the brochure that William Wrigley, Jr. once owned the island. So, what do you want to do first?"

"Well, we could double our pleasure, double our fun for starters." Jess put her arms around Devon's neck and kissed him.

When their lips parted, Devon said, "Yeah, but don't you—?"

Jess silenced him with another kiss.

Devon quickly grasped where this was going. He clutched Jess in a lover's embrace, toppling over a patio chair. They stumbled back into the room and crashed onto the bed.

***

Windsurfers, Doug Montague and Sam Warner were at Avalon Beach, fastening their masts on their sailboards, preparing for an afternoon run out on the ocean.

169

"So, Sam, getting psyched?" Doug asked.

"I don't know if I'm up for a loop just yet," Sam replied.

Doug handed Sam a helmet.

"Hey, you got the basics down. All you have to do is get on a decent reach and haul ass. When you hit the chop, tuck your body, and check your landing over your right shoulder. Once you've done it once, it's like riding a bike. You never forget."

Sam still looked unsure.

"Just go for it!" Doug said and clapped Sam on the back.

Ten minutes later, they were a quarter mile from shore.

Doug held the boom near the mast, both feet on the sailboard, the sea breeze billowing the sail.

Sam had a false start then managed to get up on his sailboard.

The windsurfers raced across the water at a fast clip.

On the first chop, Doug took his sailboard airborne and executed a perfect loop, flipping completely around. Sam followed right behind. He flew in the air and started a loop then chickened out and came down in an awkward landing.

"Take your time! You can do it!" Doug yelled, trying to build his friend's confidence while the Pacific trade winds swept them farther out onto the ocean.

***

Toby Crane, the owner of Avalon Jet Ski Rental, was finishing giving Devon and Jess last minute instructions in operating the tandem Jet Ski. Devon and Jess were wearing wetsuits and life vests.

"If you want to take a nice little run, turn right out of the marina," Toby said.

"Thanks, Toby, we'll do that," Devon said, climbing aboard the Jet Ski.

Jess sat behind Devon and put her arms around his waist while her husband started the marine engine.

Toby checked his wristwatch and said, "I'll give you a couple of minutes before I start the clock. I wouldn't go out too far. The fog will be rolling in soon. I'd hate to see you nice folks get lost out there."

"We won't," Jess said.

After a few minutes, they were out beyond the five-mile-an-hour buoy, and Devon was able to open up the throttle. They leaned into a hard right turn and blasted up the coastline. The Jet Ski bounced across the white caps doing an easy thirty miles an hour.

Devon glanced out on the ocean and saw two windsurfers sailing just below the horizon. He turned his head so that Jess could hear him over the loud engine and yelled, "Maybe tomorrow, we'll give that a try," motioning his head in the direction of the windsurfers.

The Jet Ski loomed over a swell, slammed down, and almost jarred them out of their seats.

Jess clutched the side of her jaw. "Sure, after I see a dentist and get my fillings put back in."

***

Doug and Sam decided it was time to turn back. A massive fog bank behind them gave the illusion that they were being pursued by a white tidal wave.

Luckily, the wind was in their favor and was blowing shoreward.

Sam saw a large mass two hundred feet ahead. "Hey, Doug. What's that? Looks like a capsized boat! A big one," he hollered over to his windsurfing buddy.

Doug peered through the clear plastic window in his sail. "Looks like it! Let's go see. Hey, catch this chop!"

The windsurfers sailed over the swell, looped in the air like mirrored images, and came down for perfect landings.

"I did it! I did it!" Sam screamed with joy.

Doug gave Sam the thumbs up. "See, all you had to do was just go for it!" he said with encouragement, racing toward the capsized boat.

And then Doug witnessed something bizarre.

The upended boat was moving, its inverted keel-like shape wedging through the surface swells straight for Sam.

"This is so cool," Sam yelled. "Watch this!" Sam's sailboard nosed over a choppy wave and went airborne.

Doug leaned out and peered around his sail to catch sight of his friend.

A prehistoric-looking fish—the size of a whale—leaped out of the water.

It knocked Sam off his sailboard, swallowed him up, and dove under the surface. It happened so fast Doug swore his eyes were playing tricks on him.

"Jesus Christ!" Doug shifted his weight, made an evasive jibe, and straightened his arms to fill the sail. The sailboard cut across the surface with incredible speed.

He was near enough to shore that he could make out the masts of the schooners and the yachts in the Avalon Bay harbor and the welcoming sight of the red roof on the Catalina Casino. He was so close that he could see—

The ocean rose in front of him like an underwater bomb had exploded.

He stared down the gullet of the monstrous fish and quickly joined the fate of his windsurfing buddy.

CHAPTER THIRTY-FOUR

Devon and Jess returned down the misty coastline.

"Toby wasn't kidding about the fog," Devon said, slowing down due to the poor visibility.

"Devon, look. There's something up ahead," Jess warned.

"I see it." Devon slowed and pulled the Jet Ski alongside a sailboard. The mast was broken in half, and there were splotches of blood on the Fiberglas board.

Devon shut off the engine. "Hello! Is anyone out here?"

"Can you hear us?" Jess yelled.

They drifted for a couple of minutes in the dense fog listening to the nearby waves slapping the rocky shore, but no one answered.

"We better alert the harbormaster when we get in," Devon said.

"Think we should tow in the sailboard?" Jess asked.

"Better not. Just in case someone shows up and needs it to swim back. I don't think it will drift too far." Devon started the Jet Ski and steered for the marina.

***

That evening, Devon and Jess strolled through the giant pillars that led into the Catalina Casino's ballroom. Devon was decked out in a sports jacket and slacks. Jess was radiant in a chiffon dress with thin shoulder straps, and stiletto heels.

They'd had a wonderful dinner at the elegant Avalon Grill, a dining experience that they were not accustomed to and would long remember. Devon had the grilled red snapper, and Jess had the blackened catfish.

While they were having dessert, Devon went to use the telephone and called the harbormaster to see if they were able to find the missing sailboarder. The only information readily available was that they knew the man's identity because his name was engraved on the Fiberglas board that was retrieved, and that he was an islander and was an experienced windsurfer.

The harbormaster said the police were combing the area, visiting the man's home, and questioning his friends and that if he did not materialize by the end of the night they would continue the search out in the water come daybreak.

Once back, Devon escorted Jess into the lavish ballroom. Standing on the shiny dance floor they both looked up and marveled at the beautiful red-hue walls that stretched up to the fifty-foot dome ceiling with its sparkling Tiffany chandeliers.

They walked arm in arm over to a raised seating area and sat at one of the tables.

A tuxedo band was on the elevated stage playing old-time music from the fifties.

As they held hands and listened to the melodies of bygone years, a polite waiter came by and gave them each a flute of champagne.

Devon raised his glass to toast.

"To our happy family."

"To us," Jess grinned.

They clinked their glasses together and drank.

Devon put down his glass.

"May I have this dance, me lady?" he asked jokingly.

"Why sir, I would be delighted." Jess gave her husband a curt bow of the head.

Devon scooted his chair away from the table, got up, and graciously pulled Jess's chair out for her. She held onto the crook of his arm and they stepped onto the dance floor. Devon put his right arm around Jess's waist and held her right hand in his left hand.

They danced for the best part of an hour non-stop having the time of their lives.

When the drummer ended a set with a heavy swipe across the cymbals, Jess fell into Devon's arms.

"Honey, I'm wiped out."

"Yeah, me too. That Jet Ski really must have killed my back."

"Want to hit the Jacuzzi?"

"Lead the way."

***

Sunlight filtered into their hotel room the following morning. Jess sat on the edge of the bed, surfing the channels on the television with the remote control.

"So what should we do today?" she asked.

Devon stood in the bathroom doorway, drying his hair with a towel. On the back of his T-shirt was a logo with a trout jumping out of the water within a circle bordered with the words—LAKE RECLUSE—A FISHERMAN'S PARADISE.

"I wouldn't mind snorkeling," he said and stepped back into the bathroom.

Jess turned to the TV and watched the tanned, young reporter in the white polo shirt holding a microphone. Behind him, a crowd of people were standing around an orange webbed fence sectioning off a portion of a beach.

"Yesterday," the reporter said, "a twenty-foot great white shark terrorized bathers here at Playa del Rey Beach."

Jess plucked a California map from the side pocket of her bag and unfolded it on the bed.

"Luckily for everyone," the reporter continued, "the enormous creature was already dead when it washed ashore. Judging by its severe wound, authorities believe that the shark may have been killed by a ship's propeller somewhere out in the shipping lanes."

Jess put her finger on the map and traced a short line from the beach town of Playa del Rey to Catalina Island.

"Honey, are we anywhere near the shipping lanes?"

Devon popped his head out of the bathroom. "I would guess. We're twenty-five miles from the mainland."

Jess clicked off the TV. "Maybe we better skip the snorkeling and go shopping."

"Okay by me."

CHAPTER THIRTY-FIVE

Ten Miles Off The Coast Of Santa Barbara

Of the twenty fishermen that had booked the trip, only one had become seasick on Captain Bob's Excursion cruiser.

Sitting on an ice cooler with his head between his legs, the man was taking a short reprieve before making another run to the railing. Sure it was bad enough that he had to endure the hot sun and the pitching boat, but now he was forced to stare down at the ugly rock cod that someone had pulled out of the water over an hour ago and had left on the deck as a practical joke.

Captain Bob was inside the pilot's house, manning the helm. He glanced at the fish finder and saw no sign of activity.

His first mate, Roy Harmon stepped inside and poured himself a cup of coffee.

"Good thing those guys aren't the crew or you'd have a mutiny on your hands. They want to know when you're going to stop so they can start fishing again."

"When I find—" Captain Bob paused when he saw a large blip on the fish finder screen. "Take a look at that!"

Roy glanced down and saw another large blip appear.

"What do you think, skipper? Tuna?"

"I'll bet the boat's mortgage."

"They're off the starboard bow."

They heard loud voices outside.

Captain Bob turned off the engine and put a strap on the helm to lock the wheel.

When he and Roy stepped out of the pilothouse, they saw everyone crowded together at the starboard railing. Only now, no one was speaking.

The captain and his mate squeezed between the fishermen to see what had grabbed everyone's attention.

Both Captain Bob and Roy's jaws dropped.

Out on the ocean were thousands upon thousands of dead fish, stretching toward the northern horizon, far as the eye could see.

***

Herman & Helen's Marina at the Delta's Empire Tract

Sean busily offloaded provisions from the back of the truck. He stacked a couple of heavy boxes to carry while Nell grabbed a small six-pack cooler.

"Don't strain yourself."

"Okay, I won't. Hey, I'm only a kid," Nell said and ran down the beach toward the houseboat anchored in the shallow water.

Sean peered around the top box and followed Nell, careful not to trip and fall off the brow, boarding the houseboat. They went inside the kitchen where Kate was putting things away in the cabinets and Kelly was unpacking the pots and pans.

"Gee, Mom, think you could have packed any more boxes? We're only going for five days."

"Sean," Kate said, "It never hurts to be prepared. Huh, Jonathan?"

Baby Jonathan sat in his highchair, munching on a cracker. His eyes opened wide at the sound of his name and he smiled, crumbs falling from his mouth. Max lay under the highchair, patiently waiting for something to come his way.

"Are you guys done?" Kate asked.

"There's still the fishing tackle," Sean said.

"Okay. Go ahead and lock up the truck and we'll get ready to go. I want to explore the delta before we pick up Devon and Jess at Bethel Island."

"Where are the keys? I need to lock up the utility box," Sean said.

Kate looked in her purse.

"I have them," Kelly said, dangling the keys.

"Oh, I forgot I gave them to you," Kate said.

Kelly gave Sean the keys and he left.

"You have the map of the delta, right Mom?" Nell said.

Kate pulled the folded map out from her back pocket and showed it to her smart-aleck daughter.

"For your information, I'm not going senile, and we certainly aren't going to get lost. Have a little faith. Now, go help your brother so we can leave."

Nell smirked and walked out with Max close on her heels.

"She's such a worrier, huh baby Jonathan," Kate cooed, making Jonathan laugh.

CHAPTER THIRTY-SIX

Victoria Savage stepped out of the elevator into the KHIP station's main office, located in San Francisco's Embarcadero Square. She strode down the corridor to the receptionist's desk. "I have an appointment to see Mr. Campbell."

"It's the next door down."

"Thanks."

Victoria approached the door with the nameplate Tory Campbell, KHIP News Director. She knocked, and a man's voice beckoned her in.

Campbell was middle aged with thinning hair and looked rather harried behind his cluttered desk.

"Yes, can I help you?" he snapped, not bothering to look up.

"I'm here for the interview. My name's Victoria Savage."

The phone rang and he grabbed it. "What? She didn't. I don't believe this. That's just great!" He slammed the phone down.

Victoria sat down in a chair facing the news director's desk and crossed her legs.

"You said interview," Campbell said, looking at Victoria for the first time. "For what?"

"Field reporter."

"Oh! That. Please sit down. No, you're already down. You've got to excuse me, it's been one of those days."

"I can see," Victoria said.

"I'm not usually like this. My top reporter just called in with some type of stress disorder. Incredible!"

"Can't imagine why."

"Well, just so you know, KHIP is a new affiliate. We've been broadcasting for six months now. It's been a struggle competing with the big networks, but we've managed to attract a small viewer base. Give it time. All we need is one big story. So, where did you work last?"

"KXTV in Sacramento," Victoria said.

"Hmm, good station. So, why did you leave?"

"Budget cuts," Victoria lied and flashbacked to the KXTV general manager pacing back and forth in a tyrant and what he had said to her. *"First, you almost get us sued because of that piece of yours on Senator Albright, then you get my traffic reporter killed. Not to mention a very, very expensive helicopter. What were you thinking? You're lucky I'm only firing you and not having you thrown in jail."*

"At least you left on amicable terms," Campbell said. "That's difficult in today's industry. So you decided to move out to San Francisco."

"Well, to tell you the truth, I came out here to be near my mother. She's been ill for some time. I have her in a nursing home."

"Sorry to hear that. Nothing too serious I hope."

Victoria thought back to the cemetery five years ago when she stood over her mother's grave. "It's terminal I'm afraid."

"I'm so sorry. Well, then. Seeing I have lost my star reporter, at least for the time being, would you care to take on her assignments?"

"Sure."

"Excellent. Welcome aboard. Later you can meet your camera crew. Check with Cheryl our receptionist and she'll see about getting the paperwork rolling."

Victoria stood and shook Campbell's hand.

"Thank you so much, Mr. Campbell."

"Call me Tory. Everyone calls me Tory," the news director said.

Victoria walked out of the office. She decided to use the ladies room before talking with Cheryl. She went in the opposite direction down the corridor, passing the open door of the KHIP break room. Two men were sitting at a table, drinking coffee.

Tony Carver and Bernie Barnes were just as surprised to see Victoria, as she was to see them.

"Hi, boys. Looks like the old team is back together again."

Tony sat upright in his chair. "What are you doing here?"

"Yeah," Bernie said. "We thought we'd seen the last of you."

"Sorry to disappoint you," Victoria said, and sat down at their table.

"Look, Victoria. We don't need you getting us into any more trouble," Tony said.

"He's here you know. In San Francisco."

"Who?"

"Vernon Murdock."

"Hell, Victoria. What, are you stalking this guy?"

"Better than that. I've met him. He thinks my name is Vanessa Simmons. He's even asked me out on a date."

"Does he know you're a reporter?"

"Why would he think that? Boys, there's a story here. And trust me, I'm going to get it."

Later that afternoon, Victoria went into a Kinko's print shop and used the special business card two-hour service.

***

Vernon sat at a patio table in the marina restaurant's open-air dining area and watched the sunset. He had his laptop open and newspaper clippings on the small table. When the waiter came over and refilled his coffee Vernon thanked him and resumed typing on the keyboard.

He studied the map of the Western Hemisphere on the flat screen.

A red line originating at the Galapagos Islands extended up the northern coastline of South America and onward to Latin America and the Baja leg then coursed along the beaches of southern California and ended at San Francisco.

Vernon happened to glance up as Victoria Savage approached his table.

"Hi, Vanessa."

"Sorry I'm late. Damn traffic" Victoria said, happy that her scheme was still working and that Vernon was still clueless to her true identity.

Vernon stood and closed his laptop in one motion. Victoria sat down across the table.

"Would you mind excusing me for a minute?" Vernon apologized. "Too much coffee."

"Go right ahead. It'll give me time to decide what I want," Victoria said and picked up a menu.

She glanced over her shoulder and watched Vernon enter the restaurant, and when he was out of sight, she immediately grabbed Vernon's laptop computer, spun it around and opened it.

"Silly boy, this will teach you for not shutting down. Now, let's see what you're really up to." She moved the cursor to a file named *The Silurid Domain* and double clicked.

"Bingo!"

Victoria took a diskette out of her purse, inserted it into the side of the laptop, and began copying the file. A blue bar appeared at the bottom of the screen showing the amount of the file that had been copied.

Seventy-five percent of the file had been transferred to the disk when Vernon strolled out of the restaurant.

"Oh no," Victoria said, fanning the laptop as if that would speed it.

Vernon paused for a moment to take in the stunning view of the Golden Gate Bridge with the setting sun in the backdrop.

Just as Vernon was turning to come back to the table, the bar on the computer screen stopped at 100%. Victoria closed the laptop, turned it so that it was facing Vernon's chair, but was unable to retrieve the disk.

"That's some view, eh?" Vernon said and sat down.

"Takes your breath away," Victoria replied, trying not to look guilty, fumbling with the menu. "You know what? I'm sorry, but suddenly I'm not feeling well. Could be the gas station sushi I had for lunch."

"I'm sorry to hear that. Maybe we could have dinner tomorrow at Pier 39, if you're feeling better?"

"Sure," she said and got up. "Oh, I almost forgot. I had some new business cards made up with my new cell phone number. Here, let me give you one." She opened her purse and grabbed a stack of business cards, intentionally spilling them on the patio when she went to hand Vernon a card.

"I'm such a klutz."

"That's okay, I'll get them," Vernon said.

Vernon bent down and began picking up the cards.

Victoria reached over, ejected the disk from Vernon's laptop, and stuffed it in her purse.

Vernon sat up in his chair and gave Victoria the business cards, keeping one. He looked at the card. "Vanessa Simmons. Computer Consultant. Very nice."

***

Tourists strolled up and down the crowded Santa Cruz Boardwalk amusement park. Riders screamed with each winding turn and dip, speeding along the track at 55 miles per hour on the Giant Dipper, the 5th oldest wood constructed roller coaster in the United States.

A girl perched on a porcelain horse stretched and grabbed a ring on the spinning antique carousel. People shuffled in and out of the Coconut Grove Arcade.

An audience formed on the sand listening to a live band performing a free concert on the Summertime Stage.

Out on the wharf, Cindy and Peter were standing at the railing, peering down at a seven hundred pound California sea lion basking on a ledge, its back flipper lapping in the water.

The lumbering animal looked up and barked.

"The thing's huge," Cindy said.

"Not to mention smelly. Come on, we're going to miss the concert," Peter said, taking Cindy's hand as they ran down the pier.

The sea lion barked and grunted.

Suddenly, the animal slid backward. Something beneath the surface grabbed hold of its back flipper and yanked the rotund sea lion into the water.

Cindy and Peter took the stairs onto the beach and ran across the sand. They had only gone a short ways when Peter stumbled in the dark, releasing Cindy's hand, and fell.

"Are you okay?" Cindy asked.

"What did I trip over?"

Cindy looked down. "It's a sea turtle with some crazy thing on its back."

Peter jumped to his feet. "Watch out its Michelangelo!"

"What?"

"The Teenage Mutant Turtle!"

"You're silly."

The band started a new set and the audience applauded.

"Come on, I love this song," Peter said, and they dashed across the sand.

***

An elderly couple took their nightly stroll along the beach that stretched along Herman and Helen's marina. They wore jackets to stay warm and shared their affection by holding hands.

They left the beach and walked through the parking lot.

The man noticed a glow inside the cab of a GMC truck and peered through the driver's window.

"What is it?" the woman asked.

"Oh, some fool left their phone on the seat."

"I'm sure they'll be coming back for it. Can we go in? I'm getting cold."

"Fine by me."

***

Sean sat on a lawn chair, watching his fishing pole, and listening to the chorusing crickets and frogs. The hanging Coleman lantern did a nice job of illuminating the back deck of the houseboat, but beyond the railing, everything was pitch black, consumed by the night.

Max was fast asleep at his feet. Sean raised a bare foot and kneaded Max's shoulder. The dog moaned with pleasure.

Kate and Nell could be seen through the sliding glass door, playing cards at the kitchen table.

Kelly slid open the door and stepped out onto the deck, closing the door after her. She was carrying two soft drink cans. She handed one to Sean and sat down on the lawn chair next to him.

"Thanks," Sean said, and popped the tab.

"Any luck?" Kelly asked.

Sean tapped a bucket with his foot.

Kelly peered inside and saw a black bass and two catfish.

"They like to hang out by those willows."

"It sure is peaceful out here. Though I do miss the lake," Kelly said.

"Not me. For once, I can sit and do whatever I want without Mom yelling at me to do some dumb chores. I like here just fine."

The tip of Sean's fishing rod bent over the railing.

Sean stood, grabbed the pole, and began reeling.

Kelly leaned over the railing and netted the fish.

It was another catfish.

"Man, talk about a lunker."

"Wow," Kelly said. She turned the net over and dumped the fish out onto the deck. "That's got to be over ten pounds."

"More like fifteen."

"That's one big fish."

"Come on, let's take them inside," Sean said.

"How did you do?" Kate asked, looking up from her cards as Sean and Kelly came inside.

"Come see." Sean lugged his catch into the kitchen and plopped the fish into the sink. The big cat was half in the sink and half out on the counter.

Nell dropped her cards on the table and ran over to get a closer look at Sean's fish. "That's huge!"

"They don't get any bigger than this," Sean said and proudly held the fish up for everyone to see.

Kate smiled and looked over at Jonathan, sitting in his highchair. "Look Jonathan. What's that?" she asked the infant and pointed at the fish that Sean was holding. "Say *fish*."

Baby Jonathan grinned and screeched, "Feeech!"

"Hey, Mom. He just said his first word," Sean said.

"Wait till we tell Devon and Jess. I should call them. Let me find my phone," Kate said and dashed into the bedroom.

Kelly opened the refrigerator and took out a can of baby formula. She grabbed a clean bottle and was about to pour when she thought she better give the can the sniff test. "Oooh! That's rank!"

Kate came back in the room. "Funny, it's not in there. Has anyone seen my phone?"

"No," Sean said.

Kelly shook her head.

"Oh, well. It'll show up. What seems to be the problem?"

"Jonathan's formula. It's bad."

"Dump it and open another can."

Kelly inspected the case of baby formula on the counter. "No wonder. They're all expired."

"Oh, no!" Kate said, raising her voice. Jonathan immediately gathered that something was wrong and began to bawl.

Kelly picked the baby up and tried to calm him down.

"Looks like we're going to have to make a change of plans and head over to Bethel Island," Kate said.

***

Victoria stepped out of the bathroom of her new apartment and went down the narrow hall into the tiny kitchen. She wore a bathrobe with a towel wrapped around her head turban-style to cover her damp hair. She sat down at the small table and put on her reading glasses. She inserted the diskette into the side of her laptop, waiting for the file to boot up.

Victoria's glasses reflected the scrolling images on the screen.

"My God! Is this even possible?"

A few minutes later, Victoria had retreated to her living room and was relaxing on the sofa with a glass of wine. She held up the disk and admired it as though it was the richest find in the world.

"You, my little friend, are going to win me the Pulitzer."

CHAPTER THIRTY-SEVEN

"Are you sure this is the level?" Jess asked, pulling her wheeled travel bag, searching for their vehicle in the San Francisco Airport parking garage.

"Pretty sure. There it is!"

Devon walked up to the rear of the Suburban. He opened the back and they threw in their luggage. He went around to the driver's side and unlocked the door with the Murdock Fish Hatchery logo.

Jess climbed in while Devon started the engine. He backed out of the parking space and proceeded down the ramp to the garage exit.

Twenty minutes later they were driving on Van Ness Avenue to the Marriott Hotel for a one-night stay.

"When we get to our room I'll give Vernon a call and let him know we're in the city," Jess said. "Ask him to join us for dinner."

"But I only made reservations for two."

"It won't hurt you to spend time with my brother."

"Easy for you to say."

"By the way, where are we eating?" Jess asked.

"Can't tell you."

"But how will I be able to tell Vernon where to meet us?"

"That would ruin the surprise."

Jess creased her brow and gave him an evil stare.

"Once we get to the restaurant, you can let him know."

"Why so secretive?"

"I read about this place, and it's going to blow you away. Believe me, this is going to be a night you'll never forget."

***

Twenty-six miles west of San Francisco

Vernon combed the jagged coastline of Southeast Farallon Island in his 25-foot powerboat. Heavy swells hammered the pillars of white rock. He could see the Coast Guard lighthouse up on the ridge.

A small whaler launch, with one man aboard, approached the powerboat. Both vessels bobbed like two apples in a tub.

A chomped half section of surfboard lay on the launch's stern.

"So, Dale, how's it going?" Vernon said.

"Pretty slow, I'm afraid. Haven't seen one great white in almost two days. That's unusual for this time of year. I should have been able to free tag at least two by now."

"That is strange."

"What's really strange is that there aren't even any seals around. As you know this is a big feeding ground for both sharks and seals. Can't explain it. Anyway, I better get back before the tide. Good to see you, Vern."

Vernon watched the launch head back.

He glanced down at the water. He spotted something just below the surface and leaned over the gunwale for a closer look.

A sea turtle poked its head out of the water and gazed up at Vernon as if to say hello. A black box GPS transmitter was on its back along with some scrawled numbers and the name Gorge.

"Hello, Gorge. Don't tell me you're the culprit scaring everything off." He reached inside the bait box, grabbed a sardine, and tossed the six-inch fish into the water in front of Gorge's nose. The sea turtle snapped up the offering.

"Surprised you still have an appetite after eating all those great whites." Vernon took out a spiral pad and a pen and copied down the numbers from the back of Gorge's shell. The short antenna wriggled on the GPS transmitter.

"So, Gorge, who's keeping an eye on you?"

Vernon started up the powerboat and steered for the mainland not realizing that the sea turtle was following its wake.

***

Kelly and Nell were on the flat tar-and-gravel roof of the rental houseboat, anchored in the shallows at Bethel Island.

Nell scooted onto the upper rim of the slide that stretched down to the houseboat's stern and out over the water. She pushed off without hesitation and screamed with glee all the way down. She flew out over the water making a big splash.

Wearing a pair of swim trunks, Sean climbed the ladder to the roof. When he reached the top rung, he saw Kelly lying on a towel, sunbathing in a sensuous white two-piece bathing suit.

"Oh my God, I think I'm going snow blind!" Sean said, shielding his eyes with his hand.

"Get bent," Kelly said.

"Whatever."

"Shouldn't Kate be back by now?"

"Hey, what's the rush?" Sean said and sprinted off the roof. He grabbed his knees in a cannonball on the way down and entered the water like an anvil.

A short walking distance away, Kate was in the store toting a case of baby formula in a cardboard flat over to the register. She put the formula down on the counter.

Pam Foley, the resort owner, was holding Jonathan for Kate.

"You're a lifesaver, Pam," Kate said. She opened her wallet and pulled out some bills. "I was so afraid you might not have Jonathan's brand."

"Glad I could oblige." Pam handed the infant over to Kate.

Pam took the money and rang up the sale. She handed Kate her change. "So how have you been? It's been awhile."

"It has. You know how it is, running your own place."

"Tell me about it," Pam said.

Kate looked over at a section of the store that was blocked off with sheets of plywood and asked, "Remodeling?"

"Not by choice. We had a fire in the office. Stupid coffee pot, if you can believe it. The contractor's been dragging his heels."

"Sounds like you could use a vacation. You and John should come up sometime, pay us a visit."

"I'd like that."

"I better get going. Poor Jonathan's starving. Sure wouldn't want Devon and Jess thinking I've forgotten how to look after a baby. They're supposed to meet us here tomorrow. Hey, maybe you and John would like to join us for a barbeque."

"Sounds good. Count us in. So, what are your plans for today?"

"I thought we would conserve on our gas and anchor out at Big Break."

"Have fun."

Kate had brought along a collapsible carrier with wheels for lugging the baby formula, so the trek back to the houseboat was manageable carrying Jonathan.

Once at the houseboat, Kate quickly prepared a bottle for Jonathan.

"Cool, you're back," Kelly said, opening the sliding glass door.

Jonathan cooed, suckling his bottle.

"Now that Jonathan's taken care of, we can get going. Tell Sean and Nell we'll be getting underway in about fifteen minutes."

"Sure thing," Kelly said and darted back out onto the rear deck.

***

Steve McKay sat behind his desk at the Charles Darwin Research Center, reading a report he was considering submitting when a chime on his computer alerted him to an incoming message. He looked up at his computer monitor.

A screen popped up with the words *Receiving GPS Signal.*

He typed in a code on his keyboard. A location fix came up on the screen with the exact longitude and latitude coordinates. He typed in another command, and a map of the California coast appeared on the screen. A red blip kept blinking in the inlet to San Francisco Bay.

"Gorge? What in the world are you doing way up there?"

CHAPTER THIRTY-EIGHT

Fisherman's Wharf near Pier 39

Bernie found an obscure spot by an abandoned warehouse and parked the KHIP news van. He climbed out the front of the vehicle. Victoria and Tony exited out the side door.

"I hate these assignments," Victoria grumbled.

"Jeez, all you have to do is interview the tourists. Get their opinions of Fisherman's Wharf and the attractions. Sounds like a gravy job if you ask me," Tony said, reaching into the van and taking out his camera.

"Yeah? More like a job for an intern," Victoria replied.

Tony and Bernie exchanged looks and shook their heads. After collecting their gear and locking the van, the news crew headed for the main entrance. They followed a large crowd meandering into the waterfront complex, crammed with gift shops and over a dozen seafood restaurants. A magician was performing on a stage, drawing a decent-size audience.

Victoria led the way with her microphone in hand. She spotted what appeared to be good candidates for her first interview, a family of three. They were well nourished, the pudgy son a younger spitting image of his father. The wife had ruddy cheeks, and her hair was pulled back in a fat bun. She was squinting through reading glasses at the selections on a large menu posted outside the entrance of a restaurant.

Victoria quickly announced who she was, stated her question, and shoved the microphone into the woman's face.

The surprised tourist stepped back with an indignant scowl and snarled something in German.

"Never mind," Victoria mumbled in a disgusted tone and walked off.

***

Sausalito Houseboat Marina

Vernon eased the powerboat up to the slip beside his houseboat. He cut the engine and looped a line to the cleat on the dock. The portside of the hull kissed the black tire fender. He pulled on the rope taking out the slack and secured the end around a cleat on the gunwale.

As he was climbing over the side and stepping onto the dock, something caught his eye. He walked over to the twin outboard motors mounted on the stern and looked down at the water.

It was Gorge.

"If I didn't know better, I'd say you were stalking me," Vernon said with a laugh.

The creature undulated in the saltwater current, the motion quivering the antenna on the black box attached to the sea turtle's shell.

Gorge craned his neck and looked up.

"I'll be damned. You *are* following me." Vernon took his notepad out of his shirt pocket and turned to the page where he had copied down the numbers painted on Gorge's shell.

"Stay put, I'll be right back. Now, don't go anywhere," Vernon said. He dashed across the deck and rushed inside his houseboat.

Vernon went down the hall into his office. He'd left his desktop computer on. The screensaver was goldfish swimming in a faux aquarium. He hit the space bar and the AOL menu popped up. He typed in the information he had copied into his notepad and watched as the homepage for the Charles Darwin Research Center appeared on the screen.

"Well, I'll be." He clicked on the *To Contact Us* field and shot off a short e-mail stating Gorge's current whereabouts. He figured someone was standing by on the other end and would probably respond back shortly.

He wasn't disappointed. A reply came back from a Steve McKay, thanking Vernon. Along with the response was a map of the Western Hemisphere showing Gorge's journey since leaving the Galapagos Islands—the exact route that Vernon had compiled on his laptop computer of the events that had been transpiring up the coast.

Which meant that Gorge was following the same course for some unknown reason.

Vernon sent another e-mail and inquired to Gorge's relationship to the center.

A minute passed before Steve replied. He explained the tragic events and how Gorge's mate, Maria, had been killed.

This is unbelievable, Vernon thought to himself. *Gorge's actually hunting them down. If I can keep a fix on him, he'll lead me right to them.* Vernon quickly thanked Steve and signed off.

Vernon burst out of the room and ran down the hall. He shoved opened the door but by the time he got to the dock, Gorge was gone.

"Damn." Vernon looked out over the bay. There was only another hour left before sunset. He had to find Gorge.

And then he remembered he was supposed to meet Vanessa. He hated to cancel but there was no other way. He hoped she wouldn't be too disappointed.

Then there was Jess' clandestine invitation.

He figured it best that he apologize to them in person before he took off in search of Gorge. Maybe if there was time, the four of them could plan a future dinner date.

Vernon was anxious for Jess to meet Vanessa.

He was sure they would become quick friends.

***

Devon and Jess strolled along the walkway on the western side of Pier 39 and peered down over the railing. Below were twenty or more floating platforms, each one weighted down with half a dozen sea lions. The raucous animals were a favorite tourist attraction despite their annoying barking and grunting and their pungent stench.

"I hope you don't plan eating outside," Jess said, wrinkling her nose.

"Heaven's no. Come on, we're almost there."

Soon, they were at the end of the pier. A small launch chugged toward the dock.

"So where are we going again?" Jess asked.

"Over there," Devon said and pointed across the enclosed concrete breakwater to a lighthouse on a small island.

"Weird place for an island."

"Well, it's not actually a real island. It's a floating barge made to look like an island. It has palm trees, an underwater restaurant, and a functioning lighthouse. Pretty cool, eh?"

"I'll say."

The launch cruised up to the pier where other couples and small groups were waiting.

Devon took Jess's hand as they boarded.

***

The tourists that were not dining in the Pier 39 restaurants were outside in the center of the buildings being entertained by the captivating street performers.

"What is that God-awful racket?" Victoria griped, heading down a ramp to escape the crowd.

"Sea lions." Tony looked across the bay and saw the sun setting behind the distant orange trestles of the Golden Gate Bridge. "We should be able to get some great shots with this lighting. But we better hurry."

"Good. I've got a dinner date."

"Yeah? With who?" Bernie asked.

"None of your business," Victoria snapped.

Bernie threw up his arms. "Well, excuse me."

Shouldering his bulky news camera, Tony slowly approached the railing. Bernie stayed close behind carrying the sound boom. Victoria yanked her microphone cord from Bernie's tape deck recorder so she wouldn't have to trail behind. She leaned against a marine storage locker and coiled up her cord. She stood impatiently and waited, tapping her microphone on the palm of her hand.

***

Once arriving at the man-made island everyone headed for the restaurant.

Devon and Jess decided to check out the view from atop the lighthouse, as it was just minutes away from a beautiful sunset. After climbing the spiral staircase, they went out onto the observation deck and had a glorious panoramic vantage of San Francisco's waterfront, Alcatraz Island on the bay and the Golden Gate Bridge.

"Quite the view, wouldn't you say?" Devon said.

"It's amazing."

"See, I have my moments. Wait till you see the restaurant."

"Speaking of the restaurant, I better call Vernon and tell him where we're at," Jess said and reached in her jacket pocket for her cell phone.

Devon couldn't stop himself and let out a little groan.

CHAPTER THIRTY-NINE

Bernie was monitoring the sound levels through his earphones when suddenly the volume of the sea lions rose. The cacophony of barks and wails was so deafening that Bernie stripped off his earphones. "What the hell?"

"Something's got them riled up," Tony commented, panning his camera on the overcrowded platforms teeming with agitated sea lions. A large bull barked the loudest, its platform barely afloat under the 800-pound creature. The young bulls and cows wailed.

"My God," Victoria said. "They're scared to death."

A silurid lunged out of the water, its mouth agape and bit the large bull in half with it bony jaw like a guillotine coming down on a watermelon. Gore spewed everywhere. Pink entrails gushed onto the platform. The upper section of the severed creature flopped into the water, the surface slick with blood.

"Jesus, what is that thing?" Tony yelled, capturing the footage on his camera even though there was minimal lighting as it was already sunset.

"Must be a killer whale," Bernie answered.

Tony flicked on the lamp attached to the camera housing to get a better shot but the beam did not stretch far enough to illuminate the carnage. The huge fish continued to charge across the platforms attacking the other sea lions. He could hear a loud crackling sound when the fish brushed against the other animals causing them to shudder and collapse.

"Holy shit, I think it's electrocuting the sea lions," Bernie said.

"That's crazy, killer whales don't do that," Victoria shouted. Even in the waning light, she could see that the colossus fish was a magnificent specimen. The behemoth was draped across three platforms with its tailfin still in the water, which meant that it had to be over fifty feet long—twice the length of any killer whale.

Its entire body was covered with hexagon-shaped scales that looked like armored plating. Six-foot long barbs swished about its face. In front of the massive gills were spear-like bony protrusions that the fish was using to impale and gut the sea lions.

It looked similar to the fish she had seen on the video they had stolen from the Quonset hut at the hatchery. Somehow this creature was related to that experiment, and the information she had swiped from Vernon Murdock's laptop—and now she had living proof that it existed.

"Guys! Get closer," she shouted. "That's a million dollar shot!"

***

The waiter had just seated Devon and Jess when the restaurant began to pitch and roll. Devon grabbed his water glass before it tipped over.

"What's going on?" Jess asked the waiter, staring up at the chandelier swaying over their table.

"You needn't worry. Whenever a large ship goes by, we feel the wake."

"Jess, look!" Devon pointed at a porthole high on the bulkhead of the underwater dining room that resembled the interior of a galley ship. An inquisitive sea lion peered through the glass.

"How cute."

The sea lion's face vanished, replaced by a circle of murky green water shimmering from the interior lighting fixtures.

"So, should we have appetizers while we wait for Vernon?" Devon asked.

"Sure, what do they have?"

"Well, it is mostly French cuisine," Devon noted, browsing the menu. "Feel up to trying the escargot?"

"You mean snails! Not on your life."

***

Vernon gunned the powerboat and cut through the swell. He knew the bay like the back of his hand, running at night with only silhouettes of the shoreline and navigational lights to guide him. Even though there were fewer boats to worry about, the danger of a collision on the water was greater in the pitch dark, which was why he had two halogen spotlights mounted on either side of the cockpit.

He glanced down at the instrument panel behind the helm and noted his heading on the compass. He looked over his left shoulder and saw the uninviting rocky embankment at the base of the prison buildings on Alcatraz Island.

He was looking forward to seeing Jess; Devon, not so much.

Vernon reached inside his sweatshirt pocket for his cell phone to let everyone know he was only ten minutes away from mooring at Pier 39.

**

"Are you out of your mind?" Tony yelled at Victoria.

"Keep filming!"

"It's too dark."

Most of the sea lions had clambered off the platforms, the ones that were lucky enough to escape the brutal silurid. The others were corpses afloat in the water. The salt air reeked of freshly spilt blood.

Victoria took a step toward Tony in hopes of intimidating him. "I said…"

The silurid in the water turned and gazed at the camera crew on the pier walkway.

"Ah, Jesus. Will you look at that?" Tony said.

Bernie backed away from the railing. "Let's get the hell out of here."

"Guys! It's in the water, fifty feet away," Victoria said. "It can't hurt us. Keep shooting."

Tony slipped his camera off his shoulder and held it out in front of his chest. "You want the shot so bad, you do it."

But before Victoria could react, another silurid shot out of the water like a dolphin performing a trick at Marine World—only this fish wasn't interested in a silly sardine clutched in a trainer's hand; it wanted the entire news crew.

In one quick swipe, the silurid lashed out its enormous tail and swiped Tony and Bernie into the water.

The ten-ton fish came down on the men with a thunderous splash.

Victoria screamed, dashed over, and hid behind the marine storage locker. She was shaking, huddling down in hopes of making herself as small as possible.

Her cell phone rang. "What? Not now!" The ring tone had been set at the highest volume and shrilled in the night. Victoria fumbled in her coat pocket. "Damn it, shut the hell up!" She finally got the phone out and flipped it open. She checked the screen. It was Vernon. "You got to be kidding me!"

The concrete walkway shook under her knees. She felt a blast of hot, smelly air on the back of her neck.

Victoria turned around, but before she could let out a scream, the silurid chomped down and had her upper torso in its mouth.

She kept kicking her legs.

The giant fish threw back its head and gobbled down the woman.

CHAPTER FORTY

Vernon throttled back the powerboat and drifted a hundred feet from the boat docks at Pier 39. He listened to his cell phone, hoping that Vanessa would answer, but after his call was dumped into voice mail, he decided not to press her, figuring that she still might not be feeling well. He didn't bother leaving a message.

The pier floodlights automatically came on and lit up the surrounding water.

That's when Vernon spotted the floating black shapes. He counted more than forty sea lions bobbing on the shiny surface. They were all dead; some having been brutally mutilated.

He heard a thunderous crash on the pier. People were clamoring out of a restaurant, some of them so frantic that they were falling and getting stampeded by other patrons charging outside.

An enormous head shoved through the storefront, smashing out glass, and collapsing the support beams of the structure.

Vernon instantly recognized the creature. It was a silurid. The behemoth fish was walking on its pectoral fins, thrashing its body to get out from under the crumbling building. He couldn't believe its size. It had to be over fifty feet long, maybe even sixty—twice the size of Zeus and Athena.

Frighten tourists raced through the center of the pier attraction toward the street entrance on the Embarcadero. Police officers ran in the opposite direction. At their first encounter, they drew their handguns and began firing at the massive fish. Their bullets glanced off the creature's hard-shell armor.

The silurid lunged at the men. Those that were not crushed were immediately electrocuted, their bodies flailing on the concrete.

Vernon heard a loud splash and turned. Another silurid had surfaced in the midst of the carnage of slaughtered sea lions adrift in the water.

The gigantic fish surged toward Vernon's powerboat. He immediately cranked the helm a hard right and gunned the engine. The bow passed in front of the silurid, the propeller almost striking the fish as it sounded.

The silurid on the pier scrambled off the extension and dove into the water.

Vernon heard someone call out. Two figures were standing on the seawall by a lighthouse that was swaying in the rough water. He sped over to the barrier.

"Vernon! Over here." It was Jess. Devon was with her, waving him over.

He cut the wheel and let the powerboat drift up against the seawall.

"Jump in!"

Devon helped Jess step down into the boat and hopped in after her.

"My God, Vernon! They're back!" Jess said.

"I know," he replied. He turned the boat around and sped off toward the distant lights.

CHAPTER FORTY-ONE

Devon stormed into Vernon's houseboat and stood in the middle of the living room. He didn't say anything as Jess entered but yelled at Vernon the moment he walked in. "I can't believe you knew there were more of these things out there and you didn't tell anyone!"

"Hey," Vernon said, holding his hands up in case Devon should come in swinging. "Calm down. Let me explain."

"Please, Devon," Jess said. She grabbed Devon's arm, pulled him to the couch and they both sat down.

"I wasn't a hundred percent sure, until tonight," Vernon said. "For some time, I've been monitoring strange occurrences in the Pacific, sightings if you will, wondering if it was possible that any of those eggs had made it to the ocean. When I saw a report of dead marine creatures washing ashore on the Galapagos Islands, I decided to start a timeline and began mapping a course, which eventually led right up the coast to here."

"But why would they come back?" Jess asked.

"I think they're heading for the Sacramento River."

"Why would they do that?"

"They're returning to Lake Recluse. To spawn."

"Then we have to stop them," Jess said.

"We need to get the police involved. The Coast Guard, hell, the Navy."

"I wouldn't recommend doing that, Devon. Remember back in '85, a humpback whale came into the San Francisco Bay and got disoriented. It swam up the Carquinez Strait and was heading up the Sacramento River, but got stuck in a dead-end slough. I'm sure you heard the story."

"Yeah," Devon said. "Humphrey."

"Talk about a media circus. There were boats everywhere. If that happens, those silurids will return back to the ocean and we'll never find them. Right now, they're just operating on instinct, but I don't think that will deter them from laying their eggs elsewhere. Remember, with each generation, these fish become even larger. Who knows how big they'll get next time around. A hundred feet long?"

"So, what do you suggest?" Devon asked.

"We hunt them down ourselves."

"Are you crazy? How do you propose we do that?"

"I'll show you. Come with me." Vernon crossed the room. Before opening the front door, he reached up and grabbed a key ring from a hook on the wall.

They went outside in the dark and turned down a short pier with a slip of boats. At the end of the walkway was a group of large storage sheds on firm ground.

"One of my neighbors is away attending a gun show in Vegas. He gave me his keys to watch his place," Vernon said. He stopped at one shed and fumbled with the keys until he found the right one and unlocked the padlock. He slid open the double doors, took a step inside, and pulled the light chain down.

"Oh my," Jess said.

The inside of the ten-foot by ten-foot shed looked like a sporting goods store stocked with various rifles and handguns hung on the walls; shelves brimmed with boxes containing different caliber ammunition.

There were wooden crates stacked against the rear wall.

"Is this even legal?" Devon asked.

"Probably not. He's a real gun fanatic."

"I'll say."

"Tonight, I saw some cops try and shoot one of the silurids."

"And what happened?"

"Low-caliber bullets are useless against their armor." Vernon stepped to the rear of the shed and lifted the lid off a crate that was over eight feet long.

Jess and Devon went back and looked inside the crate. A large rifle with a barrel over six feet long was inside a foam insert.

"You're looking at a Russian anti-tank rifle. Shoots 14.5-millimeter armor-piercing bullets. I think that might do the trick."

"You know how to shoot that thing?" Devon asked.

"Yeah, my neighbor's let me have a crack at it a few times."

"Oh, my God," Jess gasped.

"I know, it's a big gun but—"

"Kate and them are up near Bethel Island. They're in the path of these things. And they have Jonathan!"

"We need to warn them."

Vernon took his cell phone out of his pocket and handed it to Jess. "Here, give them a call."

Jess took the phone and quickly punched in Kate's number. She put the phone up to her ear. "It's ringing, but no one's picking up."

"This isn't good."

CHAPTER FORTY-TWO

Vernon pulled the powerboat into a slip at Pier 39, which was under a siege of pandemonium. Emergency crews and police hustled about, searching for survivors in the ruined buildings. Firemen were putting out a few fires that had erupted caused by broken gas lines.

Jess gave Devon a kiss and jumped up on the dock.

"Wait," Devon said and handed her the keys to the Suburban. "You remember where we parked?"

"Yes. You two be careful." She gave them a wave and sprinted down the boat dock.

Vernon reversed out of the slip, turned the bow, and slowly pulled away. He gunned the powerboat out into the channel once he passed the 'SLOW 5 MPH' buoy. He glanced down at the GPS tracker mounted on the console.

"Is that a fish finder?" Devon asked.

"More of a sea turtle finder."

"How's that?"

Vernon told Devon about the Charles Darwin Research Center and that they were tracking the goings-on of a particular sea turtle named Gorge.

"My hunch is that Gorge has been following the silurids. I believe he'll lead us straight to them."

"Let's hope so."

***

Jess had heeded the traffic report warning of a long delay due to an accident involving a big rig tanker spill on Highway 101 going north. She decided to backtrack across the Golden Gate Bridge and catch Interstate 80.

What she had not anticipated was the retrofitting on the Bay Bridge. Ever since the Loma Prieta earthquake in 1989 caused one of the bridge's upper deck sections to collapse when the bolts were sheared off, the structure was heavily monitored with preventative maintenance.

Today was no exception. Due to some repairs, only one eastbound lane was open, causing a glutted bottleneck.

After almost thirty minutes of stop-and-go traffic, she was finally off the bridge and proceeding up the North Bay on the interstate.

She was just passing the outskirts of Berkley when she happened to glance down at the gas gauge.

The needle was drastically close to empty.

She had ten more miles before the turnoff for Highway 4 and maybe another twenty miles to Bethel Island.

As much as she dreaded to stop, she had to choose an exit and fill up, which meant yet another costly delay.

***

"Gorge's signal is coming from inside that slough," Vernon said and pointed at the narrow inlet.

He took the boat slowly up the restricted channel.

The mud flat banks on either side were covered with salt marsh growth, a combination of tall reeds and scraggly brush that reached up to heights of ten feet in some places.

After less than a mile, the inlet came to a dead end.

The thick brush had thinned out, and there was a massive U-shaped mound of sedimentary mud that had built up into a ten-foot high horseshoed wall and could have easily been mistaken for a levee.

Devon spotted something on the muddy bank.

It was a little black box.

Vernon saw it, too. "It's Gorge's transmitter. Must have fallen off."

"Now what?"

***

Jess turned into the parking lot and pulled up in front of the Bethel Island store. She got out of the Suburban and went inside.

"Hello," she said and walked up to the woman standing behind the counter.

"Hi there."

"My name's Jess McNeeley. I was wondering—"

"You must be Kate's daughter-in-law. It's so nice to finally meet you. I'm Pam Foley. Kate and I have been friends for years," Pam said. "In fact, she was here not too long ago."

"She was?"

"Had to pick up some baby formula. For your little boy."

"Do you have a way that I might reach them? A ham radio perhaps."

"No, I'm sorry," Pam said, and gestured to the boarded-up wall on the other side of the store. "Our radio was destroyed in a fire."

"Do you have any idea where they were headed?"

"Big Break. Kate said they were going to anchor there for the day. If you're lucky, you might spot them from the frontage road."

"Thanks, I appreciate it. Nice to have met you," Jess said, and dashed out of the store.

***

Kelly was excited to be able to drive the houseboat. There were no other boats around, none that she could see out the sliding glass door. She kept her speed to ten knots and was especially careful.

Baby Jonathan was sitting in his highchair, eating Cheerios scattered on his tray. As always, Max was close by, waiting for something to come his way.

Kelly saw a jetty creeping up and steered clear of the boulders jutting out of the water like granite icebergs and brought the bow around into an obscure cove.

A few seconds later, the houseboat shuddered and jolted to an abrupt stop.

The sliding glass door opened and Sean poked his head in. "What did you hit?"

"I don't know," Kelly said.

Kate and Nell hurried into the kitchen.

"I'm sorry, Kate, I don't know what happened."

"No, no it's my fault. I completely forgot," Kate said.

"Forgot what?" Kelly asked.

"To check the tide table. It must be low tide. We've run aground."

CHAPTER FORTY-THREE

Devon had taken the helm so that Vernon could set up the anti-tank gun at the bow of the boat. The muzzle extended two feet beyond the handrail. A tote pan full of six-inch long armor-piercing cartridges was on the deck next to the mighty single-shot gun for quick access when Vernon needed to reload.

There was no telling how far the search would take them so Vernon had brought along six five-gallon cans of gasoline so that they could refuel on the go. The gas cans were strapped at the rear of the boat, butted against the transom.

While they were in the shed, they had decided to increase their firepower and helped themselves to an M-16 carbine with 20-round clips, an M-1 Garand rifle that held 8-round clips, and what Vernon called "a showstopper," one M-31 anti-tank rifle grenade launcher, all of which were vintage weapons used during the Vietnam War.

Devon had put a strap on the M-16, which was slung over his shoulder hanging on his back.

Vernon confessed that he had never fired the grenade launcher but understood how it operated and saw no harm in bringing it along. There were some missile-shaped grenades in a box, along with a detachable spigot-type grenade launcher that fitted to the muzzle of the rifle. If need be, the M-1 Garand could also be adapted and used to propel grenades.

Vernon had hoped that he could assume a prone position while firing the big gun as it packed quite a wallop, enough recoil to snap a collar bone if the stock wasn't properly tucked in the shoulder, but unfortunately, there wasn't adequate space for him to sprawl out. Plus, the gunwale was too high.

Instead, he propped the inverted V-shaped gun stand on a wooden crate so that he could kneel down behind the gun. For padding, he planned to use a life vest to minimize the kickback. He'd also brought along safety glasses and a pair of ear protectors.

He was feeding a single cartridge into the breech when Devon shouted, "Straight ahead. I think I see them!"

Vernon gazed out over the bow. At first glance, they looked like migrating whales, their backs slightly visible, skimming just under the surface.

Devon pushed the throttle forward. The powerboat leveled out and raced up the channel. "I'll get as close as they'll let me. Then try and get off a shot."

Vernon signaled that he understood. He put on his safety glasses and ear protectors.

He knew it would be difficult getting off a clean shot with the boat bouncing over the water.

The powerboat edged up on the silurids.

Vernon grabbed the handgrip and slipped his finger inside the trigger guard. He used his other hand to clutch his upper arm to steady his shot.

He aimed at the silurid to his left, and when he'd lined up his target, pulled the trigger.

Even with the ear protectors, the gunshot was deafening, sounding more like a cannon. The stock slammed into his shoulder.

Vernon raised a pair of binoculars to see if he had hit the mark. Blood was gushing out the gunshot wound on its rear flank, leaving a trail in the water.

"I don't believe it," Vernon yelled. "I hit it!" He was surprised how unremorseful he felt, even if the fish were offspring of Zeus and Athena.

The silurids suddenly veered course and headed toward land.

"Where're they going?" Devon yelled over the din of the engine.

Vernon followed the silurids with the binoculars and focused the lens on the cove up ahead. "They're heading for Big Break."

He scanned the shoreline and saw a houseboat down near the bend. Adjusting the magnification, he could just make out the three figures standing by the stern railing. "Ah, Jesus."

Vernon quickly inserted a cartridge into the chamber of the anti-tank rifle.

He looked back at Devon and yelled, "GUN IT!"

***

Sean stood waist-deep in the murky water. He adjusted his diving mask and dove under the houseboat while Kate, Kelly, and Nell watched from the rear deck.

Baby Jonathan could be seen through the sliding glass door, snacking as usual in his highchair while Max sat patiently at his side.

After about thirty seconds, Sean surfaced.

"Well, how bad is it?" Kate asked.

"The prop is stuck in the mud, but I can't tell if it's bent," Sean said, slipping off his mask.

"I guess we have no choice but to wait until the tide comes in," Kate said.

"Yeah, if we try and start the engine, we'll damage it for sure."

Kate turned her head. "Wait a minute, I think I hear a boat. Maybe they can give us a tow out to deeper water." She gazed up the shoreline, spotting the powerboat. "There it is!"

And then she saw the two monstrous shapes in the shallows.

CHAPTER FORTY-FOUR

The two silurids swam into the four-foot deep shoal, their bodies no longer submerged, bellies skirting the rocky bottom. They quickly turned and rose up on their pectoral fins to face their pursuer.

Devon steered the powerboat directly at the gigantic fish. "Take your shot!"

Vernon targeted the already-wounded silurid and pulled the trigger. The big gun bucked making a loud boom. This time, the bullet struck the fish above the right eye, shearing off a plate of armor and gouging out a chunk of white flesh. Blood streamed out of the ragged hole. Even though it should have been a serious injury, the fish didn't seem fazed.

Vernon started to reload when Devon suddenly cut the wheel. The other silurid was charging at them, skimming across the water. The massive fish struck the starboard side of the boat like a battering ram and flipped the craft over on its side. Vernon and Devon flew out of the boat, crashing down a few feet from the shore.

"Get out of the water," Vernon yelled, wading hurriedly to shore. He spotted the M-1 Garand lying on the sand and picked it up.

Devon scrambled to the rocky bank. He flipped the strap around and aimed the M-16, firing off a quick burst at the closest silurid. The bullets were useless; it was like expecting BB pellets to punch through steel.

The injured silurid attacked the capsized boat like it was a live adversary while the other humongous fish steadily advanced on the men.

***

Kate heard gunfire off in the distance.

"What was that?" Nell asked.

"Hey, we're not near a military firing range, are we?" Kelly asked.

"Everyone, get inside," Kate said. "Quick."

Sean climbed up the short ladder onto the deck and grabbed a towel.

Kate opened the sliding glass door, but before they could enter, Max bolted out of the kitchen and ran pass them. The dog dashed across the deck and vaulted over the railing into the water.

"Max! Come back here!" Kate yelled.

"What's gotten into him?" Kelly asked.

"Where the heck's he going?" Sean rushed over to the railing. He watched Max splash through the shallow water then run up onto the bank, disappearing around the rocks.

***

Devon heard a dog barking and looked down the shoreline. He couldn't believe it.

"Max!" he shouted. "Get away!"

The golden retriever saw Devon and barked a greeting.

Devon glanced across the water in the direction Max had come from and spotted the houseboat less than a half a mile away down the shore.

Max stepped toward the tail of the silurid closest to the men. The dog yelped and jumped back, feeling electric current radiating off the fish. He ran up on the rocks and began barking, taunting the monstrous fish.

The fifty-foot silurid turned on its pectoral fins and glared down at the dog. It opened its mouth, and let out a guttural groan.

"Max, get out of there!"

The silurid thrust its tail and lunged for the dog.

Max spun around and bounded through the water in the direction of the houseboat.

The fish was incredibly fast, gliding over the shallow water.

Devon glanced back at Vernon.

Vernon waved him on. "Go! Save your family!"

Devon dashed after the silurid chasing Max.

**

Sean was looking through a pair of binoculars, watching the ordeal unfold further up the shore from atop the houseboat. "Mom, you're not going to believe this. It's...oh shit!"

Kate looked up from the aft deck. "Sean, haven't I told you never—?"

"You don't understand!" Sean shouted, still staring through the binoculars. "I can see Max and he's running this way! And there's this giant...holy shit! It's chasing Max! They're heading for the houseboat!"

Kate gazed up the shoreline. "My God, you're right. You kids get back!" Kate ushered Nell and Kelly inside and partially closed the sliding glass door.

Inside the kitchen, baby Jonathan was sitting in his highchair, enjoying the show, enthralled by the images on the other side of the sliding glass door like watching an exciting TV episode on a big screen.

Max was galloping through the shallow water and being chased by a scary fish the size of a school bus.

Baby Jonathan laughed and squealed, "Feeech...feech." He clapped his tiny hands, associating what he believed to be Max's newfound playmate.

Max clawed his way up onto the transom, scampered across the deck. He used his nose to nudge open the sliding glass door enough for him to squeeze through.

Soaking wet, he immediately shook, spraying the baby.

Then Max turned in a protective stance and stood in front of the highchair.

The silurid leapt out of the water, sailing straight for the sliding glass door.

"Max, run!" Kate shouted, snatching baby Jonathan out of his highchair. She tucked him under her arm like a running back would a football and dashed back through the houseboat.

The silurid plowed headfirst into the kitchen like a wrecking ball.

The dining room set and surrounding furniture were crushed under the enormous weight. The houseboat keeled to one side from the impact.

Sean was lifted off his feet and sent rolling across the gravel and tar roof.

He managed to cling onto the air-conditioner housing or else he would have fallen overboard.

He scampered across the rooftop and looked over the edge.

Below, the giant fish was squirming to free itself, shaking the entire houseboat like a fierce bull trying to dislodge its head out of a fence.

Sean couldn't believe his eyes. This was just like the fish that had chased him and Nell on Grizzly Island—only twice as big!

Even with its head and shoulders shoved inside the houseboat, there was still more than forty feet of body and tail protruding out over the transom onto the water.

The houseboat rocked under his feet like shifting seismic plates. It was like trying to keep his balance at the epicenter during a reeling earthquake.

The fish was gradually backing its way out of the houseboat. It was only a matter of time before it would break free and attack again.

Sean heard someone shout his name.

He looked beyond the fish's thrashing tail and saw Devon running along the shore toward the houseboat.

Before the boy could reply back, he heard a truck roaring down the frontage road.

As it approached, Sean realized it was the Suburban with Jess behind the wheel.

Sean was about to raise his arm to wave when Jess suddenly veered the truck off the road and went airborne over the embankment.

The Suburban smashed into the silurid's shoulder blades, driving the front grill and most of the hood deep into the creature's armored flesh.

CHAPTER FORTY-FIVE

Sean climbed down from the roof and ran forward. Devon jumped up on the deck.

"I smell gas," Sean said, grabbing the handle but the door wouldn't budge. The hood and fenders had buckled rearward, crushing the door panels, and wedging the doors in tight so that it was impossible to get them open.

Devon was on the other side of the vehicle. He could see Jess pressed back against the seat and appeared to be unconscious.

Luckily, she had been saved by the airbag. The inflated canvas was already slowly losing shape.

"Jess, can you hear me?"

"We have to get her out of there," Sean said.

Devon knelt and stole a peek under the truck.

Gas was leaking from the tank. A small trail of petroleum was running down a crease in the silurid's armor and forming a puddle under the hot engine block, ticking like a time bomb about to go off.

The creature's enormous bulk shifted.

"It's still alive." Devon stood. He made a fist with his left hand and held it with his right for power and drove his left elbow like a piston into the glass of the driver's door. The safety glass crumbled into the interior of the SUV.

Devon reached in and pushed the deflated airbag against the steering wheel.

He fumbled around and found the release to Jess's seatbelt buckle. Jess was beginning to come around.

"Sean! Make sure everyone gets off the houseboat."

"Sure you don't need me to help?"

"Go before it blows."

Sean jumped down and ran along the side of the houseboat.

Devon grabbed Jess under the arms and hoisted her out through the smashed out window frame.

Flames shot up from under the truck.

CHAPTER FORTY-SIX

Vernon could hear the water crackling as the silurid shoved against the damaged powerboat. The monster fish was only twenty feet away. He raised the M-1 Garand, aimed for the head, and shot three times. One of the bullets struck it in the left eye. A white, milky goop spurted out. The silurid shook its head as if doing so would ease the pain.

He was about to take another shot when he noticed the five-gallon gas cans strapped to the boat. He thought if he could puncture one of the cans, the boat would explode and blow the fish to pieces.

Vernon targeted one of the cans and fired. When the bullet punched a hole in the container, Vernon ducked expecting the boat to blow up. Gas leaked out and flowed in the water, creating an oily film on the surface.

He tried firing four more times, each shot hitting a different gas can, but still the result was the same; just more gas funneling out.

He glanced around the water. There were some dead fish floating on the surface, a couple life vests, an orange case…

Vernon rushed over and snatched up the marine distress kit. He opened it up. Inside was a flare gun, along with four aerial signal flares.

The silurid charged.

Vernon stuffed a flare into the gun, fired at the gas cans, and dove behind a large rock.

A wave of heat rolled over him with a loud concussion; fiery flames rose fifty feet into the air. Burning chunks rained down.

Fragmented boat pieces and bloody fish gore splattered the water and shore.

***

As Devon struggled to help Jess down to the deck, he heard the distant explosion and saw the cloud of smoke up the shoreline.

They jumped into the shallow water and scrambled ashore to the embankment.

Kate was standing on the frontage road with baby Jonathan in her arms. Sean had gathered up Kelly and Nell. They watched anxiously as Devon and Jess made their way up.

A scorching hot blast seared the air.

Everyone ducked when the gas tank on the Suburban blew up in a fiery plume of smoke, igniting the silurid in a roaring ball of flames. The fire swept through the houseboat and ignited both the fuel tank and the propane canisters.

The houseboat erupted in a hail of zinging shards like a grand fireworks show.

Everyone stayed flat on the ground until the last piece finally settled to earth, before getting up.

"How am I going to explain the houseboat?" Kate asked, passing baby Jonathan over to Jess.

"You could always say you had an accident in the kitchen," Jess said.

"Yeah, say we were having a big fish fry," Sean said, and everyone broke out laughing.

Jess turned and gazed down the frontage road.

A lone figure was walking toward them.

Jess raised her arm and waved.

Vernon waved back.

CHAPTER FORTY-SEVEN

San Francisco Bay—A Few Days Later

"I can't believe I let you bring me out here again," Cindy said, shivering on the tailgate of Peter's truck.

"What, don't tell me you'd rather be sitting in some stuffy theater watching a crappy movie?" Peter said, his attention on his surf pole staked twenty feet away on the rocky shore.

"Duh yeah," Cindy replied. "Some guys actually take their girlfriends out on a proper date."

"Well, I'm not like *some* guys, now am I?"

"You're telling me."

The wind had picked up forming white caps on the bay.

A faint clang sounded in the night.

Peter was scooting off the tailgate when Cindy grabbed his arm.

"It's a buoy, silly."

"Oh, yeah, you're right," Peter said, realizing that the sound was coming from somewhere out on the bay and not the bell attached to the tip of his fishing pole.

"I wish you'd get as excited about me as you do with your fishing," Cindy said.

"What...?" Peter said.

"I said—"

"No, what's that?"

"What's what?"

"That," Peter said and pointed. "Out there, in the water."

"I don't know," Cindy said, squinting.

"Look, there's more." Peter grabbed the flashlight out of his tackle box and jumped down off the tailgate. "Come on, let's get a closer look."

Cindy slid off the tailgate.

They held hands and carefully stepped across the rocks, following the beam of the flashlight. Small waves lapped onto the rocks.

Peter and Cindy climbed up on a large boulder and stared down. Peter shined the light on the water.

"Holy shit!" Peter shouted. Cindy clenched his arm.

"Why is the water all red? Is that blood?" she asked.

"Nah, it's a red tide. Some kind of plankton."

"So what are those things floating on the water?" Cindy gasped.

"Jellyfish."

***

Galapagos Islands—San Cristobal Island—Six Months Later

Steve McKay strolled along the sand to the base of the boulders then scaled the rocks up to a ledge that overlooked the ocean.

A sea turtle was on the beach, laying her eggs in an indentation in the sand.

She scooped sand over her eggs with her back flippers, burying them for protection against predators.

The name *NINA* was painted on her shell along with a series of numbers. A black GPS transmitter was affixed to her shell.

Slowly but determined, she pulled her way through the sand.

Gorge was waiting for her at the water's edge.

Together, they emerged into the curling surf.

Steve watched the twosome paddling out into the waves.

He gazed at the horizon long after the sea turtles had submerged, marveling at the spectacular splendor of the setting sun sinking into the sea like a fiery ingot.

END

CHECK OUT OTHER GREAT DEEP SEA THRILLERS

MEGATOOTH
by Viktor Zarkov

When the death rate of sperm whales rises dramatically, a well-respected environmental activist puts together a ragtag team to hit the high seas to investigate the matter. They suspect that the deaths are due to poachers and they are all driven by a need for justice.

Elsewhere, an experimental government vessel is enhancing deep sea mining equipment. They see one of these dead whales up close and personal...and are fairly certain that it wasn't poachers that killed it.

Both of these teams are about to discover that poachers are the least of their worries. There is something hunting the whales...

Something big.
Something prehistoric.
Something terrifying.
MEGATOOTH!

BLOOD CRUISE
by Jake Bible

Ben Clow's plans are set. Drop off kids, pick up girlfriend, head to the marina, and hop on best friend's cruiser for a weekend of fun at sea. But Ben's happy plans are about to be changed by a tentacled horror that lurks beneath the waves.

International crime lords! Deep cover black ops agents! A ravenous, bloodsucking monster! A storm of evil and danger conspire to turn Ben Clow's vacation from a fun ocean getaway into a nightmare of a Blood Cruise!

CHECK OUT OTHER GREAT DEEP SEA THRILLERS

SEA RAPTOR
by John J. Rust

From terrorist hunter to monster hunter! Jack Rastun was a decorated U.S. Army Ranger, until an unfortunate incident forced him out of the service. He is soon hired by the Foundation for Undocumented Biological Investigation and given a new mission, to search for cryptids, creatures whose existence has not been proven by mainstream science. Teaming up with the daring and beautiful wildlife photographer Karen Thatcher, they must stop a sea monster's deadly rampage along the Jersey Shore. But that's not the only danger Rastun faces. A group of murderous animal smugglers also want the creature. Rastun must utilize every skill learned from years of fighting, otherwise, his first mission for the FUBI might very well be his last.

OCEAN'S HAMMER
by D.J. Goodman

Something strange is happening in the Sea of Cortez. Whales are beaching for no apparent reason and the local hammerhead shark population, previously believed to be fished to extinction, has suddenly reappeared. Marine biologists Maria Quintero and Kevin Hoyt have come to investigate with a television producer in tow, hoping to get footage that will land them a reality TV show. The plan is to have a stand-off against a notorious illegal shark-fishing captain and then go home.

Things are not going according to plan.

There is something new in the waters of the Sea of Cortez. Something smart. Something huge. Something that has its own plans for Quintero and Hoyt.

CHECK OUT OTHER GREAT
DEEP SEA THRILLERS

THEY RISE
by Hunter Shea

Some call them ghost sharks, the oldest and strangest looking creatures in the sea.

Marine biologist Brad Whitley has studied chimaera fish all his life. He thought he knew everything about them. He was wrong. Warming ocean temperatures free legions of prehistoric chimaera fish from their methane ice suspended animation. Now, in a corner of the Bermuda Triangle, the ocean waters run red. The 400 million year old massive killing machines know no mercy, destroying everything in their path. It will take Whitley, his climatologist ex-wife and the entire US Navy to stop them in the bloodiest battle ever seen on the high seas.

SERPENTINE
by Barry Napier

Clarkton Lake is a picturesque vacation spot located in rural Virginia, great for fishing, skiing, and wasting summer days away.

But this summer, something is different. When butchered bodies are discovered in the water and along the muddy banks of Clarkton Lake, what starts out as a typical summer on the lake quickly turns into a nightmare.

This summer, something new lives in the lake...something that was born in the darkest depths of the ocean and accidentally brought to these typically peaceful waters.

It's getting bigger, it's getting smarter...and it's always hungry.

CHECK OUT OTHER GREAT DEEP SEA THRILLERS

PREDATOR X
by C.J Waller

When deep level oil fracking uncovers a vast subterranean sea, a crack team of cavers and scientists are sent down to investigate. Upon their arrival, they disappear without a trace. A second team, including sedimentologist Dr Megan Stoker, are ordered to seek out Alpha Team and report back their findings. But Alpha team are nowhere to be found – instead, they are faced with something unexpected in the depths. Something ancient. Something huge. Something dangerous. Predator X

DEAD BAIT
by Tim Curran

A husband hell-bent on revenge hunts a Wereshark...A Russian mail order bride with a fishy secret...Crabs with a collective consciousness...A vampire who transforms into a Candiru...Zombie piranha...Bait that will have you crawling out of your skin and more. Drawing on horror, humor with a helping of dark fantasy and a touch of deviance, these 19 contemporary stories pay homage to the monsters that lurk in the murky waters of our imaginations. If you thought it was safe to go back in the water...Think Again!

Printed in Great Britain
by Amazon